BRAWL!

Buck came off the floor with both hands filled with sawdust, which he hurled into Longarm's face. When Longarm tried to clear his vision, Buck hit him with a thundering overhand that drove Longarm over another card table and sent him skidding across the sawdust.

"Damn," Longarm swore groggily as Buck swung a boot at his face. Longarm rolled sideways and felt the wind move beside his cheek. He could have drawn his gun, but Longarm had a strong urge to see if he could whip this big bastard with his fists.

"You had your chance," Buck snarled, throwing himself at Longarm before he could stand . . .

TABOR EVANS

LONGARM

AND THE
COUNTERFEIT CORPSE

JOVE BOOKS, NEW YORK

LONGARM AND THE COUNTERFEIT CORPSE

A Jove Book / published by arrangement with
the author

PRINTING HISTORY
Jove edition / August 1996

All rights reserved.
Copyright © 1996 by Jove Publications, Inc.
This book may not be reproduced in whole
or in part, by mimeograph or any other means,
without permission. For information address:
The Berkley Publishing Group, 200 Madison Avenue,
New York, New York 10016.

The Putnam Berkley World Wide Web site address is
http://www.berkley.com

ISBN: 0-515-11925-3

A JOVE BOOK®
Jove Books are published by The Berkley Publishing Group,
200 Madison Avenue, New York, New York 10016.
JOVE and the "J" design are trademarks
belonging to Jove Publications, Inc.

PRINTED IN THE UNITED STATES OF AMERICA

10 9 8 7 6 5 4 3 2 1

Chapter 1

Although it was a gorgeous afternoon in Denver with the autumn leaves in full color, U.S. Deputy Marshal Custis Long was scowling as he marched east on Colfax Avenue. A plump and out-of-breath clerk struggled to keep stride with the big and angry marshal as they passed the rows of brownstones and business establishments.

"Dammit!" Longarm swore, glancing back at the puffing, red-faced clerk. "I told Billy Vail that I have a train to catch this afternoon for Cheyenne. I've paid for my ticket, and I'm all ready to go on vacation!"

The clerk, charging forward to overtake Longarm, gasped, "Mr. Vail is well aware that you have not had a vacation in almost three years and that you are way overdue for some time off, but this seems to be an emergency!"

Longarm glanced up as a flurry of colorful leaves

sailed across the Colorado state capitol grounds. Fifteen miles to the west, a dark bank of clouds was gathering over the Rocky Mountains. Longarm knew that a storm was brewing and that there would soon be heavy thundershowers. He'd expected to miss them as he enjoyed the first leg of a long train ride that would eventually take him to Boston, where a certain lady was expecting to entertain him. And, while Longarm did not normally go east for any reason, this young socialite was especially charming and generous with her assets.

As they neared the corner of Colfax, Longarm had to stop and wait for a carriage of women to unload. They were laughing and clearly out for a little shopping and entertainment. One of them, a voluptuous blonde, stared boldly at Longarm. He should have tipped his hat to her in a silent salute, but he was in such a foul mood, all he could do was manage a curt nod. The ladies passed and the clerk plucked at Longarm's sleeve.

"What?" Longarm growled.

"Your legs are about four inches longer than mine, Marshal Long, and I'm half running to keep up with you. Could you just slow down a little?"

"You said this was an emergency."

"Oh, it is! In fact, the governor himself might be in attendance."

"Governor Ganzel?"

"Yes! As well as the head of the entire federal Department of Justice, Commissioner Malcomb Hall."

Longarm halted in mid-stride and turned to confront the clerk. The United States deputy marshal was a big, rugged man. At six-four with craggy features and a John L. Sullivan mustache, Longarm gave the impression of being tall, tough, and weather-beaten. His imposing pres-

2

ence was usually tempered by the friendliness in his eyes, but today even that was absent. His eyes were gunmetal gray and frosty today.

"All right, Duncan," Longarm growled. "You *must* know what this is all about. 'Fess up!"

Duncan shrank back. "Listen, Marshal," he whined, "Mr. Vail swore me to secrecy. He said I'd be fired if I told you what was going on down at the federal building."

Longarm grabbed the man by the lapels of his coat and raised him to his toes. "Duncan," he said, his voice low and threatening, "what would you rather be . . . fired or strangled to death?"

"I'm just following orders. You know I'd tell you what was up if I could."

An old woman wearing furs and an emerald broach tapped Longarm on the back with her umbrella. "You!" she said sternly. "Unhand that poor little man this very minute and stop acting like a big bully!"

Longarm released Duncan, who retreated beyond his reach and tried to regain his composure.

"What is the matter with you!" the old lady demanded. "You're twice that little fellow's size! Shame on you for scarin' him so badly."

"He's a worm," Longarm pronounced. "A petty little bureaucratic worm who was sent to stop me from taking a well-deserved and long-overdue vacation."

"From what?" the woman demanded, her voice stern and accusing.

"I'm a United States marshal," Longarm said.

"I don't believe it!"

"He is," Duncan said. "But he's not one of our *nicer* ones."

"Shut up!" the old lady snapped, not taking her eyes off Custis. "If you indeed are a federal officer, then perhaps there is some justification for your poor behavior. I abhor criminals, and I suppose that catching and bringing them in to face justice takes a hard, brutish man."

"I was going to vacation in Boston and hoped to soak up some culture and address that personal shortcoming," Longarm said. "But I've just been sidetracked."

The old lady snorted. "Well," she said for a parting word, "then why don't you just ignore the 'worm' and go on to Boston as you'd planned!"

"I can't. I like my boss and my job."

The old woman banged the tip of her umbrella on the sidewalk. "Then do your duty and quit whining! Boston will wait, and besides, I suspect that there is no hope whatsoever of turning you into anything approaching a gentleman."

"Thanks," Longarm grumped as the old lady turned and marched off down Colfax. "Thanks a lot!"

Longarm turned back to take his ire out on Duncan, but the little paper-pusher was nowhere in sight.

"I could just go catch my train," Longarm mused aloud. "But that worm Duncan would tell Billy and the governor that I ran out on them and I'd be in a hot kettle of water when I got back. Might even be out of my job."

Longarm wrestled with his dilemma for only a moment. Then he continued on toward the federal building. The Boston lady, whose name was Miss Emily Underwood, would just have to wait a few extra days for his long-anticipated arrival. If anything, it might cause her to welcome him with an even greater passion than he'd already expected.

Longarm went straight into the federal building and

wasted no time greeting acquaintances as he strode across the immense foyer with its marble floors. Marshal Billy Vail greeted him at his office door.

"Thank God you didn't have time to catch that train," Billy wheezed as he led his best deputy marshal into his office. Before he closed the door, he said to Duncan, who had suddenly appeared from behind a bookcase, "Don't let *anyone* inside until this meeting is finished. Understand?"

"Yes, sir, Mr. Vail!"

"Good." Billy dredged up a smile. "Custis, thanks for coming so quickly."

"My train is leaving within the hour. I'd still like to be on it." When Billy didn't respond, Longarm said, "That *is* a possibility, is it not?"

"This way," Billy said as they moved into his office, which was large and afforded a splendid view of the Rocky Mountains. Only now the curtains were drawn and there were three other men waiting.

"Marshal Long," Billy said, beginning the introductions. "I'm sure you know Governor Ganzel and our executive officer, Mr. Malcomb Hall."

"I do," Longarm said to both men, who had not bothered to rise and were studying him closely. "It's a pleasure."

"You may not feel that way after this meeting," the governor warned. "We're in quite a fix, and Mr. Vail assures both myself and Commissioner Hall that you are his very best deputy marshal. A real problem-solver."

"A doer, the one man who could handle this job," Commissioner Hall added. "That's how Mr. Vail described you, Marshal Long."

"I am flattered," Longarm said, expecting that he

5

would soon pay dearly for these compliments. "What seems to be the problem?"

"Have a seat," Billy said, offering Longarm a stiff-backed wooden chair while all the rest of them rode fine leather upholstery. "It will take a few minutes to explain the mess we are in and try to acquaint you with all the facts leading up to the predicament."

"Yes," Governor Ganzel said, "I'd like to hear them myself. I'm still not sure how this could have happened."

"There were some serious problems with security, Governor," Malcomb Hall said.

"And who takes responsibility for that!"

"I do," the commissioner said, completely unruffled by the governor's bluntness. "But there is never any sure way to stop someone in a position of trust who goes bad."

Oh, God, Longarm thought, *this is going to be even worse than I'd expected.*

"Well," Billy said, taking a seat behind his desk and steepling his short, stubby fingers. "I suppose I should begin at the beginning."

"Brevity," Longarm advised, thinking how his train would be leaving the Denver station in exactly forty minutes and there was still a shred of hope he'd be on it if he could find a way to decline this assignment. "Brevity is always appreciated."

Billy was a rotund, soft-looking fellow who had once himself been a very effective marshal. He was physically unimpressive, entirely forgettable, but had proven himself to be extremely cunning, courageous, and resourceful. Longarm did not like to take orders from anyone, but he considered Billy a friend and so that made things a good deal easier all the way around. Having himself been in the field, Billy understood the problems of the deputy marshals who worked under his supervision and he would vigorously defend them when they occasionally fouled up.

"Well, Custis," Billy said, leaning back in his chair. "We have a little problem over at the Denver mint."

"A *little* problem?" Longarm challenged.

"Hell, Billy, tell him the truth. We have a big, *big* problem!" the governor exclaimed. "A million-dollar problem!"

Longarm's eyebrows shot up. "A *million dollars*?"

"If we're lucky," the governor of Colorado said, looking slightly pale. "You see—"

"Perhaps it would be better if I explained," Commissioner Hall interrupted. "I have just learned a few more details within the last hour."

"Of course. You explain," the governor said.

Hall ran his hand across his eyes, and Longarm guessed that despite the commissioner's calm demeanor, he was a man under a great deal of pressure. "To begin with," Hall said, "we had no idea that the old plates had been stolen, much less the paper, ink, and—"

"Whoa!" Longarm said. "What old plates and what paper and ink?"

"I'm sorry," Hall said, "we received new plates, ink, and instructions from Washington, D.C. to begin printing a slightly different hundred-dollar bill at our Denver mint. The new currency was going to make it even more difficult for counterfeiters. The changes in the new hundred-dollar bills are readily evident only to the trained eye. We studied them carefully and followed the Treasury Department's instructions—to the letter."

7

"I'm sure you did, Commissioner," the governor said with a perfunctory air, "but how your people could be so lax about the old plates defies all understanding."

"We weren't lax!" Commissioner Hall lowered his voice and dragged his handkerchief out to dab at his haggard face. "We weren't lax. All the standard procedures were taken to insure that the old plates and inks were catalogued and destroyed."

Governor Ganzel, an immense figure prone to hysterics, jumped to his feet and cried, "But they *weren't,* dammit!"

Billy Vail also came to his feet. "Gentlemen, there is no use crying over spilled milk. It is obvious that the plates were not *all* destroyed and now we have to find out who took them and who is using them."

"How," Longarm said, still not sure he understood exactly what the problem was, "do you know that they weren't all completely destroyed?"

"Very simple," Billy said, reaching into his desk drawer and drawing out a bundle of crisp new one-hundred-dollar bills. "These were deposited at the Great Northern Bank of Cheyenne four days ago. They are the discontinued currencies using the obsolete plates."

"How—"

"Without training, the only way you'd know they were illegal are by the serial numbers," Billy explained. "Their sequence has been discontinued. We have, in effect, someone out there who has taken it upon himself to become a *second* United States Treasury. His highly mobile mint deals in nothing but hundred-dollar bills."

"Thank God it wasn't a plate for thousand-dollar bills," Governor Ganzel said glumly.

"They would have been far, far too conspicuous," the

commissioner interjected. "We'd have nailed the counterfeiter right away. Thousand and five-hundred-dollar bills attract a lot of attention."

"That's probably true," the governor said. "But hundred-dollar bills are quite common, even among the riffraff and your ordinary gamblers."

Longarm came to his feet and crossed the room to stand before Billy's desk. "May I see those bills, please?"

"Sure," Vail said, handing them over to him. "There are an even hundred in that stack. Ten thousand dollars."

Longarm whistled softly as he hefted the crisp new bundle. "I've never held that much cash all at once."

"They are supposed to be worthless. Illegal," Commissioner Hall said with annoyance. "But . . . unless you know the discontinued serial numbers or have a trained eye, those bills cannot be distinguished from all the millions of dollars in previous hundreds that have already been issued."

"Then you'd better get a list of serial numbers out right away," Longarm said, "because I know that I could sure spend this bundle in a hurry."

"Of course you could," the commissioner sighed. "And because it was our blunder, anyone accepting that currency would have every reason to expect that it is legitimate. They could, we are quite sure, sue both the federal government and the state of Colorado for damages and reimbursement."

"It could bankrupt Colorado," Governor Ganzel whispered.

"It could bankrupt the feds too," Commissioner Hall assured them. "I can tell you this much—a special secret service courier is being rushed to Washington, D.C., this very moment to advise our President of this mess. And unless I am very much mistaken, he is going to hit the ceiling. When that happens, we *must* have the thieves and those outdated hundred-dollar plates back in our possession.''

Hall looked around at them, his eyes settling on Longarm. ''You were recommended for the job. Can you do it?''

''Well,'' he answered, hearing the first blast of the whistle announcing the Boston train's departure, ''I'm better at just going after your ordinary murderer or—''

''*Can* you do it!'' Governor Ganzel demanded. ''Because, if you have any doubts—''

''He can do it,'' Billy Vail interrupted. ''If anyone can find the thief, or thieves, it's Deputy Marshal Custis Long.''

The officials stared at Longarm, who finally nodded. ''I can do it,'' he heard himself say.

All three of his superiors relaxed. The governor was the first one to ask the question that was on all their minds. ''Where do you start and how fast can you put a stop to the production of these bogus bills?''

''I don't know yet,'' Longarm admitted. ''I'll have to be briefed and then pick up a trail and—''

''We can help with that,'' Commissioner Hall snapped. ''Our in-house investigation has revealed that the plates were supposed to be destroyed exactly ten days ago. We have the signed order saying that they *were* destroyed.''

Longarm came to his feet. ''Signed by?''

''According to our manual of procedures, when plates are destroyed, two signatures are always required,'' Hall

10

explained. "Two men were given the responsibility and signed the completion order."

Longarm glanced at Billy, then back at the commissioner. "All right, where can I find and question them?"

"One is in the morgue," Billy said softly. "And the other has . . . vanished."

"Vanished?"

"That's right," Commissioner Hall bristled. "His name is Nathan Cox. He was a six-year employee of the Denver mint and had an excellent performance history. He was already a supervisor and a real 'comer' in the organization. He was well liked and dedicated."

"Dedicated to committing a multimillion-dollar larceny," Longarm growled.

"Please don't say that!" Governor Ganzel begged. "Perhaps Mr. Cox has printed only a few hundred thousand. Even Colorado could stand that kind of loss . . . if it were shared by the federal government."

"Of course it would be," Hall said. "At least, I'm sure that the President would recognize that these were federal employees even though—"

"Gentlemen," Billy Vail said, cutting off the discussion. "These are matters that need not be covered now. What we need to do now is to find Nathan Cox."

"How did the other signer meet his end?" Longarm asked.

"His neck was broken and witnesses are sure that his last visitor was Mr. Cox."

"Who has not," Longarm said, "been seen since."

"That's right," Billy replied. "Federal officers have searched his apartment and found nothing. All of Nathan Cox's friends have been brought in for interrogating and have not been able to tell us anything."

11

"What about relatives?" Longarm asked.

"The man was a loner," Hall said bitterly. "Cox had a lot of women friends, but he never let them into his apartment or shared his confidences or personal life. Those who have been questioned say that Nathan Cox was very, very slick."

"What does that mean?"

"It means that he is a ladies' man," the commissioner answered. "Here is his picture. You can see that Cox is very handsome. He's also quite a talker. The women we questioned simply could not believe that Nathan Cox could have committed any crime."

"With one notable exception," Billy interjected. "A woman by the name of Miss Diana Frank. She says that she finally saw our thief's dark side and would not be surprised at anything that he might do—including murder."

"I'd like to speak with her," Longarm said. "She obviously saw through this man's con game."

"I'll give you Miss Frank's address, but she's already been questioned at some length," Hall said. "I'd think you'd want to go to Cheyenne, where the first large batch of bogus bills appeared."

"I will go, but the next train—"

"You'll have a *special* train," the governor interrupted.

"A train of my own?"

"Of course," Governor Ganzel said, managing a stiff smile.

"One question," Longarm said. "Why aren't dozens of men searching for Nathan Cox?"

"They are," the governor admitted. "But none of them knows *why* we are so desperate to apprehend the

12

turncoat and destroy those old treasury plates.''

''Why all the secrecy?''

Hall looked at Billy Vail. ''You explain it to him. He's your chosen one.''

Billy nodded. ''Custis, with those plates, special paper, and ink, even a marginally talented editor or pressman could run off millions of dollars worth of new hundred-dollar bills.''

''I understand that, but . . .''

''And,'' Billy continued, ''if word of what Nathan Cox has in his possession became common knowledge, we fear that Cox would become the most hunted man in America, and many of the hunters would not employ the highest ethical standard.''

Longarm nodded as he began to understand the enormity of the problem. And the fact that he alone had been given this private, potentially explosive inside information made him feel a little overwhelmed.

''I would suggest,'' Billy Vail said, dragging Longarm out of his somber reverie, ''that you go to interrogate Miss Frank this very hour and then pack and be at the train station within—''

''Two hours,'' Longarm said. ''I'll need at least that much time.''

''We'll give you one and a half,'' Governor Ganzel said, jumping to his feet. ''And we'll give you another three days to apprehend Mr. Cox.''

''You can give me three days or three weeks,'' Longarm said, ''but it may take three months if Cox has already left Cheyenne and is on the run. If he went east it will take me longer to track him down in those big cities.''

"We think he went westward," Commissioner Hall said.

Longarm folded his arms across his chest. "Why?"

"Because Nathan Cox was raised on a cattle ranch somewhere near Prescott, Arizona. Those we've questioned say that he talked constantly about his family's ranch. Apparently, his father made some very unwise investments a few years ago and the ranch was foreclosed."

"And you think that Cox intends to go to Arizona and buy back his ranch?"

"It's a real possibility."

"A very *obvious* possibility," Longarm said. "If the man is smart and ruthless enough to have planned out the theft and then broke his partner's neck, I doubt he'd be stupid enough to be predictable."

"Unless," Billy said, "he does think with his heart as well as his head."

"I'll need photographs and a file on everything you can put together on Nathan Cox. I want to know his personal likes and dislikes. How he spends his free time and—"

"He doesn't believe in free time," Hall said. "He's either chasing women or bedding them."

"Or gambling," Billy said. "He likes poker and faro. I'll bet that even as we are speaking, he's gambling away our money."

The governor nodded. "Or in bed with a beautiful woman and tickling her with ... well, what else but crisp, new hundred-dollar bills?"

Longarm started for the door. "What kind of woman is Miss Frank?"

"A looker, like all the others that attract Nathan

14

Cox," Commissioner Hall said. "She's tough, so don't expect to get her to open up with any new information. I think you're wasting your time and ought to just leave for Cheyenne."

"He could save us money by catching the regular train to Cheyenne," the governor said hopefully.

"No," Billy Vail insisted. "Marshal Long really does need to interrogate Miss Frank. The savings would be minimal."

"Are you kidding!" the governor exclaimed. "It will cost the citizens of Colorado at least five hundred dollars to put your deputy on a private train and rush him to Cheyenne."

"You never worried about the expense during your last campaign," Commissioner Hall snapped.

"That's uncalled for!" Ganzel erupted.

"Gentlemen!" Billy Vail cried. "This is not the time or the place for wrangling."

"Mr. Vail is right," Longarm said, "and I'll carry out the investigation my way, or you can find another man."

Malcomb Hall's cheeks blazed. He was Billy Vail's boss and could have raised a stink, but instead, he clamped his jaws shut and let Longarm hurry away to find Diana Frank.

Chapter 2

Diana Frank's apartment wasn't exactly in a seedy part of town, but it certainly didn't qualify as being upscale either. The brownstone was showing signs of early decay, and Longarm saw that there were several vacancies in the building. Her apartment was numbered fourteen, although Longarm doubted that there were anywhere near that many units.

Longarm hurried inside and down a long, dim hallway. The apartments all had big white letters on their doors but when Longarm knocked at number fourteen, there was no answer.

"Damn!"

He knocked louder, and a small dog began to bark in the adjoining apartment, number nine. Longarm knew that he had to have some answers, so he banged on that door as well until he heard the rattle of a chain and the door opened a crack. The muzzle of a little dog burst

16

through the opening at ankle level. It tried to bite Long-arm, who would have kicked the little bugger if a heavy-set woman hadn't pressed her cheeks to the crack and stared out at him.

"What do you want?" she asked, her eyes taking Longarm in from his boots to the flat crown of his snuff-brown Stetson. "My, my, you're a big one, aren't you?"

Longarm removed his Stetson and tried hard to ignore the yapping, snapping little mongrel who was actually foaming at the mouth, so intense was its desire to bite. The woman was middle-aged with dyed blond hair and dressed in worn pink pajamas. Longarm could smell whiskey fumes strong enough to anesthetize flying insects.

"My name," he said, fishing into his brown tweed suitcoat and then vest, "is Deputy Marshal Custis Long. I've got a badge in here somewhere, if I can just find the damned thing."

"Don't worry about it," the woman said. "My name is Rose. Would you like to come in?"

"I don't have time," Longarm said. "I'm looking for Miss Frank. Can you tell me where she has gone?"

"Moved out this morning."

"No."

"Yes, and I'm glad. You should have seen all the men she had trooping in and out of this building!" Rose winked. "And I'll tell you something else, Marshal, they didn't come to talk about the weather."

"No," he said, "I don't suppose they did. I didn't realize that Miss Frank was that kind of woman."

"Well," Rose said, dropping her voice to a whisper, although they were alone in the hallway, "let's just say that Miss Diana Frank was not a pillar of virtue and that she didn't audition for the church choir. I, on the other hand, have very high moral values . . . on most issues. Are you married, Marshal?"

"Ah . . . yes," Longarm lied.

Rose had little porcine lips and now they formed a pout. "Too, too bad," she said, her smile dying. "Otherwise I might just be interested in getting better acquainted."

"I *must* find Miss Frank."

"Why? Was she *that* good?"

"Actually, I . . . I have a package for her."

Rose's blue eyes lowered to his sides. "I don't see one."

Longarm was getting annoyed. "I really do need to find her quickly, Rose. Can you help me?"

"Oh, all right. If Diana isn't visiting her best friend, you might try the saloon in the hotel just down the street. It's called Hannigan's. That was Diana's favorite hangout when she wasn't visiting with her best friend."

"I know the place."

"I used to go there too," Rose said, making a face. "But the people just got too high-toned. And the bartenders, they all wanted tips and tried to push all that expensive stuff on you so that the joint could increase its profits. You know how those places are."

"Yes, but . . ."

"They like to think that they cater to the upper crust, but they don't. Not really. They just overcharge the regular people, the ones that kept them in business."

"Did you ever see this man come here," Longarm said, slipping Nathan Cox's picture through the crack in the doorway.

Rose giggled. "Oh, sure! Nathan was just as snooty

as Diana. Wouldn't hardly give me the time of day. A real ass, but awful handsome. Like you, Marshal. Sure you wouldn't like to come in and join me in a drink or two?''

"Unh-unh," Longarm said. "I'm married, remember?''

"Oh, yeah. Well, there are marriages and then there are marriages.''

"Where does Miss Frank's best friend live?''

Rose returned the picture. "How bad *do* you want to know, big boy?''

The woman's eyes and tone of voice left no doubt as to the fact that she was no choir girl either. "Not *that* bad," Longarm said, starting to leave.

"Oh, all right!" Rose called over the yapping of her dog. "Diana's best friend Beverley lives in apartment six, just down the hall.''

"Thanks!"

"Don't mention it," Rose said, kicking her little mutt away from the door and then slamming it hard.

Longarm banged on Beverley's door until it was opened. After introducing himself, he said, "It's very important that I find Diana Frank as soon as possible. I understand that she moved out but that you were her close friend.''

"That's right," Beverley said, leaning up against the doorjamb smoking a thin black cigarette. "Diana went to borrow some money so that she could buy a ticket on the next train to Cheyenne. In the meantime, she's staying with me. What do you want to see her about, Marshal?''

"About a man named Nathan Cox.''

Beverley made a face that did nothing to improve her

looks. "That sonofabitch was as crooked as a snake. He *used* Diana. Promised her the world. Said that he was going to come into some big money and that they'd get married and he'd take her back east."

"But he didn't."

Beverley dropped her cigarette on the hallway rug and stomped the life out of it with her heel. "Hell no! Cox ran out on Diana with a pocketful of her money. That's why she's leaving Denver. It's been painful and she's bitter. Besides that, I kind of think she wants to find and then kill the smooth-talking sonofabitch."

"What for?"

"Castration."

Longarm blinked and started to laugh, until he saw that Beverley was serious. "Well," he said, "before she tries that, I need to find him first."

"Is he in trouble?"

"Yes."

"Big trouble?" Longarm knew that the woman wanted him to say yes, but he wasn't about to say too much and certainly not spell out the charges. "Well, ma'am, let's just say that Nathan Cox might be spending time wearing stripes."

Beverley clapped her hands together, obviously pleased. She was wearing a baggy housedress and Longarm could see that she was the kind that could fix herself up to look pretty nice if she cared to.

"So, Cox really did something important, huh?"

"Yep."

"He worked for you guys at the mint. Right?"

"Correct."

"What did he do, steal a wagonload of new cash?"

"I can't say," Longarm told her. "It's all under investigation."

"Well, good luck on finding him," Beverley said. "He's as slippery as an eel, and he could probably sweet-talk his way through the pearly gates into heaven. But he's no damn good, and beneath all that sugary pap he's got a vicious streak as big around as your leg. I've seen him when he gets mad and he can be dangerous."

"When do you expect Miss Frank to return?"

"At any time, if she didn't stop at Hannigan's."

"I think I'll go there and then come back if she's still missing."

"Don't let Diana get drunk and spend whatever money she managed to borrow. She's in a bad frame of mind right now, thanks to lover-boy Cox. But she'll survive and, if she finds that snake, he'll be damn good and sorry he ever broke her heart and took all her savings."

"Thanks for your help," Longarm said, turning to leave.

"Are you married?" Beverley called.

"Uh . . . yes."

"Too bad. You're just the kind of man that could make Diana forget about Nathan."

Longarm didn't know what to say about that, so he just tipped his hat and hurried outside.

He found Diana Frank at the hotel saloon. She was seated at a back booth with two young men, and they were all laughing and having a little party. But when Longarm came to a halt beside their table, the two men glared up at him.

The bigger man growled, "This is a private party, mister. Butt out."

"Miss Frank," Longarm said, ignoring the remark,

"I'm sorry to interrupt, but I'm Deputy Marshal Custis Long and I need to talk with you privately."

Diana was a tall, willowy beauty with lustrous brown hair and almond-shaped green eyes that absorbed Longarm like a bar rag. She smiled loosely and said in a slurred voice, "Draw up a chair and join us for a drink, Marshal. I like to be surrounded by handsome men."

"I have to talk with you in private."

The big man said, "Why don't you come back some other time, Marshal. The lady has all the company she needs right now."

"That's right," the other man, shorter but squat and powerful with a pitted face, said. "So why don't you just look her up tomorrow."

"I have to talk to her now," Longarm said. "So both of you get out of here and leave us alone."

"Now, wait just a damn minute!" the bigger man exploded, bouncing to his feet. "We've done nothing wrong and you can't just march into this place and start ordering people around like you're some kind of gawd-damn king."

Longarm tried to curb his anger. "Mister, I'm here on official business, and I've asked you in the nicest way I can to leave. I won't ask you again."

"Better leave, Joe," Diana said, her loose smile fading. "You too, Tom."

"I never did like lawmen," Tom spat out. "Bunch of bossy bastards who—"

Longarm's fist traveled a mere four inches before it stabbed into Tom's gut. The short, stocky man's eyes bugged and his lower jaw sagged as he gasped for air. The big man started to swing, but Longarm grabbed him by the shirtfront and slammed him up against the wall so hard, the saloon shook and the back-bar glasses rattled.

"Joe, don't say a word. Just grab your little friend and get out of here before I lose my temper," Longarm warned.

Joe was dazed, but he had enough sense to grab his friend and propelled him toward the saloon's exit. Everyone in Hannigan's stared, but Longarm ignored them as he slid into the booth beside Diana Frank.

"I'm sorry to have ruined your party," he said.

Diana swept back a strand of her lovely hair and smiled. "It was going to be *their* party, not mine."

"Do you really need traveling money *that* bad?"

"Yes," she said, emptying her glass. "Buy me another?"

Longarm wanted the woman to be clear-headed, but he knew that he dared not decline her a drink. "Sure," he said, signaling to the bartender.

"How did you know that I needed 'traveling' money?" she asked after the bartender brought them both whiskeys.

"I talked to your friends at the apartment. Beverley told me that you were planning to leave Denver."

"Did she tell you why?"

"She did," Longarm said. "We're *both* looking for Nathan Cox. That's why I came to find you. I thought maybe we could help each other."

Diana smiled and then she wagged her finger in his face. "Just how could we do that, Marshal?"

"I need to find him in a hurry. You want to find him too. Maybe we can pool our information and find him together."

"He took every dollar I could beg, borrow, save, or

23

steal and ran away with it,'' Diana said, bitterness creeping into her voice. "It was my fault. I should have known better than to trust a man like Nathan.''

"Everyone makes mistakes.''

"I make a career out of misjudging men,'' Diana said morosely. "I never seem to learn how to pick them.''

She took a drink and looked into Longarm's eyes. "Why do you want to find Nathan?''

Longarm just had a feeling that he could not fool this woman and any attempt to do so would badly backfire. "We think he also took some of the taxpayers' money, Miss Frank.''

"He took a whole lot more of yours than mine, didn't he,'' she said with a smug little smile.

Longarm leaned across the table. "What makes you think so?''

She leaned back. "Got a cigarette?''

"No.''

"Cigar, then?''

"Yeah, but they're not exactly the kind a lady would enjoy and—''

"I'm certainly no lady,'' Diana said, her anger flaring. "So, Marshal, let's just cut the damn flattery! I heard enough sweet-talking bullshit from Nathan Cox to last me a lifetime.''

"All right.'' Longarm kept a couple of nickel cheroots in his coat pocket, more for chewing than smoking. But now he brought out two and slid one across the table to Diana.

They both bit off the tips and Longarm struck a match with his thumbnail. "If you're ready to talk, Miss Frank, I'm ready to listen.''

"It's a sad, sad tale of betrayal,'' she said. "I loved

the man. I really did. He'd worked for the Treasury Department for a lot of years, had nice friends and seemed to be a solid citizen. I thought that he was . . . well, a big, big cut above the pair that you just threw out of here.''

"He fooled the government too," Longarm said. "If that's any consolation."

"Not much. How much did he take the mint for?"

"We don't even know yet," Longarm said. "But it could be a . . . fortune."

"Jeezus!" Diana cussed, slamming her fist down on the table so hard, whiskey spilled from their glasses. "I was afraid of that. So," Diana asked, leaning back in her chair and studying him with slightly unfocused eyes. "Exactly what would you like me to tell you?"

"It's real simple, I want to know where I can find Nathan Cox."

Diana stared for a moment, then she shook her head. "And if I did help you, what would I get out of it for my trouble?"

"Revenge."

"Not enough," she said. "Not nearly enough. I can get revenge without the government's help. In fact, the kind of revenge I'm looking for would be illegal."

"He's going to prison for a long, long time," Longarm said. "I don't think that you want to do the same. You're still a young and beautiful woman."

"Not so young and not so beautiful. Anyway, don't flatter me, remember?"

"Sorry." Longarm exhaled a cloud of blue smoke up toward the ceiling. "What do you want from us in addition to the apprehension and long-term imprisonment of Nathan Cox."

"Torture him?"

"No can do."

"All right," she said, "I want my money back. All of it! And I want a lot of interest besides."

"How much did he steal from you and how much interest?"

"He took me for three thousand dollars. I want ten from you, Deputy Marshal Long."

"That's pretty steep interest on your money."

"I got a feeling that it's chicken feed compared to what Nathan has taken the government for. Am I right?"

Longarm wondered how Commissioner Malcomb Hall and Governor Ganzel would take to this blackmail. And then he remembered the anxiety in their voices, their offer for a private railroad car, and their dire, if overstated, predictions of bankrupting the state and possibly even the federal government if Nathan were allowed to churn out bogus hundred-dollar bills.

"I think ten thousand dollars is acceptable."

"All right, then that means it is worth twenty."

"No," Longarm said, "it is not."

"Twenty thousand," she said, her eyes turning as hard and bright as emeralds. "Ten thousand up front before I tell you where he's gone, and another ten thousand when he is arrested."

"I don't think you can help us that much," Longarm said, pushing to his feet. "You're too greedy."

"Sit down!"

Longarm sat. "Fifteen thousand. Half now, half when he's apprehended. What do you say?"

"I can ask," Longarm said. "That's all I can do. I haven't the authority to make that kind of a deal."

"Who will you ask?"

"Governor Ganzel and Commissioner Hall."

"Then ask them and bring me seventy-five hundred if they want to find Nathan Cox in their lifetimes," Diana told him. "If I don't hear from you by this evening, I'll just figure that we're each on our own and may the best person find the thieving sonofabitch first."

"You're a tough woman, aren't you?"

Diana Frank blew smoke in his face. "Tell the bartender on your way out the door to send a bottle of his finest whiskey over to this table, on the federal government."

Longarm pushed to his feet. "One thing we need to understand right now, Miss Frank. If you don't have the answers we need to grab Cox before he does any more damage, you wouldn't be allowed to keep the seventy-five hundred."

"Fair enough."

"All right, we're going back to your friend Beverley's place. She's worrying about you and you've already had enough to drink. You're no good to yourself and you're no good to us if you're drunk."

The woman started to say something, then seemed to change her mind. "All right," she said, pushing to her feet. "Take me out of here, Marshal. But you know what?"

"What?"

"You're pretty tough yourself."

"I have to be."

"So what is my excuse?" she asked.

"Too many bad men?"

"Yeah," Diana said. "That's for damn sure. "Are you any good, Marshal?"

"Nope."

Diana stared at him for a moment, and then she started to laugh as he led her out of Hannigan's.

"What's so funny?" Longarm asked as they stepped outside.

"At last, a man who is both handsome *and* honest!"

Longarm had to chuckle. "I'm not above telling a lie or two," he admitted. "For example, I told your friend and Rose down the hall that I was married."

"But you're not?" Diana looked up at him, her expression serious.

"No," he said. "I am not."

"Good," she said, slipping her arm around his waist and pressing her hip against his for support as they walked down the street. " 'Cause you know what?"

"What?"

"I think we could be friends."

"There's just no time for that right now," Longarm said. "After I get your money, I'm going to be hitting trail and driving hard until I apprehend Cox. Hell, Diana, the governor has even promised me a special train. It's the one that he uses when he campaigns for political office."

"Dammit!"

"What?" he asked.

"I should have asked for a *hundred* thousand dollars instead of settling for just fifteen."

"Maybe," he said as lightning cracked across a dark and ominous sky and the rain began to pour down on Denver.

It was midnight when Longarm returned to the apartment building where Diana Frank was staying with her friend Beverley. The two women were drinking coffee. A big,

28

half-eaten pumpkin pie rested on the table between them.

"You're soaking wet," Beverley said. "It's a real drencher out there."

"Have you got my money?" Diana called from across the room.

"Seventy-five hundred dollars payable only if you can tell me where to find Cox."

"Sit down," Beverley said. "I'm going out for a while."

"In this weather?"

"I'll be fine," she said. "I don't want any part of this and I suspect that it's all secret business."

"That's true."

Diana gave her friend a hug and helped her into a heavy coat. "This won't take long. Good-bye."

"Good-bye?"

"I'll see you again," Diana promised.

Beverley glanced at Longarm. "She's not going to be putting her life in danger, is she?"

"No."

"All right."

As soon as Beverley was gone, Diana said, "How about a slice of pie?"

"No thanks."

"You need something to eat because we have a long trip ahead of us, Marshal."

"What do you mean 'we'?"

"I'm coming with you."

"No!"

"Then the deal is off," she said, finishing her coffee and walking to the coat rack, where she began to work into her own heavy coat.

"Where are you going?" Longarm asked.

"I'm disappearing, of course. I'll find Nathan and kill him myself."

"And that's worth fifteen thousand dollars and prison?"

"I think it is, yes."

Longarm shook his head. "I've never come across anyone as stubborn and pigheaded as you are, Miss Frank."

"Together, or separate. Which is it going to be, Marshal Long?"

"Together."

"Good!" Diana brightened. Her green eyes were a little bloodshot but still beautiful, and now that their differences had been settled, she seemed to take on fresh inner resources. "Let's go?"

"Where?"

She looked at him with surprise. "Why, to the train station so that we can ride Governor Ganzel's private car, of course."

"Well . . ."

"But first, the money."

"No," he said. "First information."

"All right," she said. "Nathan Cox went west."

"To what was once his family ranch near Prescott, Arizona?"

She looked amused. "Is that what you think?"

"Yeah," he said, "it is."

"Then you're wrong."

"So, where is he going?"

"You'll find out," she said, extending her hand for the cash, "just as soon as I'm paid and we ride that special train."

Longarm gave the woman the seventy-five hundred

dollars that his desperate superiors had been more than happy to provide and then, before he could ask any more questions, Diana swept out the door and he chased her through the rain all the way to the Denver Pacific Railroad yards.

Chapter 3

"The governor is waiting for you inside his special coach," Billy Vail said as Longarm and Diana hurried through the downpour and the muddy train yard. "Be warned that he's not in a very good mood."

Longarm growled. "I'm not in a very good mood either, but that isn't going to cause Governor Ganzel to lose any sleep. By all rights I should be riding a first-class seat to Boston and sipping on a little brandy."

"Good evening, Miss Frank," Billy said, ignoring Longarm's complaints. "I'm sorry that you had to come out in this bad weather."

"I don't mind," Diana said. "It will be a real treat to ride up to Cheyenne in the governor's coach."

Billy's jaw dropped. He swung his eyes to Longarm. "Nothing was said about Miss Frank coming along with you."

"I know," Longarm said. "It just sort of happened."

"Well," Billy groused, "I suggest that you make it *unhappen!*"

"Not a chance!" Diana shouted. "I'm going with him, or the deal is off!"

The rain began to pour down on them, so Longarm grabbed Diana's arm and pushed her forward. "Can we argue about who's going and who's staying *inside* the coach?"

"That's fine with me," Diana said. "Is Governor Ganzel inside?"

"He is."

"Then let's go join him!" Diana said, bounding up the steps to the coach's platform.

"The governor isn't going to be pleased about having her in his coach," Billy said, leaning close to Longarm's ear. "He isn't even happy about *you* using his coach."

"Tough shit," Longarm said, cold, wet, and feeling used. "He can call the whole thing off anytime and I won't complain."

"The governor and Commissioner Hall aren't close friends, but they stick together, and that could cost me my job," Billy said. "So, unless you want a new boss, you might just try to bury your sentiments."

"All right," Longarm said grudgingly, "I'll behave."

"Thanks."

The inside of the special coach was plush, with lots of deep-blue velvet curtains and upholstery, brass, and mahogany. Longarm had been inside it only once, and then for just a moment as he'd delivered a message to the governor. But this was altogether different.

"Wow!" Diana squealed as she bounded inside and out of the rain. "What a place!"

The governor as well as three of his aides and Commissioner Hall were huddled together over drinks and conversation. Diana's entry made them forget whatever they were plotting. The governor was a well-known womanizer in his own right, and now he sprang to his feet, staring at Diana, who managed to look appetizing despite the fact that her wet hair was plastered around her face and her eye makeup had run down her cheeks.

"Well . . . hello," the governor said, reaching for a drink. "No one told me you were coming!"

"Life is full of surprises," Diana said before she smiled and added, "And you are far more handsome than I had been led to believe, Governor."

Governor Ganzel seemed to almost slump with relief, and he grinned stiffly. Commissioner Hall rolled his eyes upward, and Billy Vail looked as if he were going to be ill as Diana waltzed forward and took the governor's hand, saying, "I've always been such an admirer. I feel as if we've known each other . . . somewhere, somehow."

"Really?" Ganzel gulped. "I don't think that's possible. Unless we met on the street just in passing."

"That *must* be it," Diana said, gazing past the men to admire the plush interior of this special railroad coach. "And it's going to be such a pleasure to ride up to Cheyenne in your personal coach, Governor."

"Now, wait a minute!" Commissioner Hall said, coming to his feet. "This is a federal investigation, and we can't allow civilians to be involved. It could be dangerous."

"Oh," Diana said, "I'm very much aware of that, Commissioner. But, you see, Nathan Cox was once an actor. I'm sure that your background search revealed that, didn't it?"

"Uh . . . no," the commissioner stuttered. "I wasn't aware that he was an actor."

"A very good one," Diana assured them. "So, you can well expect that he will have dramatically changed his appearance. I believe you'd have an impossible time identifying Nathan without me. You see, he may change the way he looks, but he couldn't change his voice or the way he moves. I'd notice those things instantly. That's why I'm sure you understand why it's imperative that I accompany Deputy Marshal Long to Cheyenne."

Diana looked to the governor, who was pouring himself a stiff drink. "Don't you agree, Governor?"

"Oh, yes!" Ganzel said, tossing whiskey down his gullet. "By all means, go to Cheyenne."

"I shall," Diana said. "And what about you, Governor? Are you coming to Cheyenne with us?"

"I can't. Affairs of state, you understand."

"Of course."

"I should go," Commissioner Hall said. "We've people in Cheyenne already and—"

"Malcomb," the governor said, "I'm sure that we *both* have pressing matters to attend to right here in Denver, and our engineer says the locomotive has a head of steam and this train is ready to roll north."

"But—"

"Malcomb," the governor said, an edge creeping into his voice. "Why don't we just let these people be on their way. I'm sure that Deputy Marshal Long has everything in control. Isn't that right?"

"Sure," Longarm said, totally baffled by what had happened between the governor and Diana Frank yet delighted that the brass was remaining in Cheyenne. "Everything is under control."

"Excellent!" the governor said, tossing down his drink and rushing for the door.

Commissioner Hall was furious and Billy Vail was just as mystified as Longarm about what had transpired between the governor and the lady. The mystery, however, was solved the moment the train started to roll.

Longarm removed his dripping overcoat and headed for the bar. He was cold and confused.

"You're probably wondering what happened between me and the governor," Diana said as she watched him pour three fingers of expensive Kentucky bourbon.

"Yeah, I am," Longarm replied, taking a gulp and savoring the warm, delicious flow of liquor so much, he smacked his lips. "I expected a real dogfight about your coming on this trip."

"I suppose I should have explained a few things before we arrived, but we were in such a rush."

"You have a lot of explaining to do, Diana. You see, neither the governor nor the commissioner were very happy when I talked them into paying you fifteen thousand dollars."

"Well," Diana said, "as you might have guessed, the governor and I are old friends."

"Is that a fact?"

Diana went over to the well-stocked bar and examined its contents. "Oh, yes," she said, "I've even been in this coach a few times. Nothing has changed but the faces. The governor still insists on the best liquor money can buy, thanks to the generosity of his political supporters."

"Why don't you just quit dancing with me and spell it out plain," Longarm suggested.

"All right, Marshal. I've not only *met* Governor Ganzel, but I've also spent some intimate hours with him on this coach.''

Longarm just shook his head. "The governor is married now. I can't imagine that he would have agreed to work with you given this background.''

"He knew me as Miss Diana Frost," she explained, pouring a crystal tumbler full of brandy and then sinking down on one of the blue velvet couches.

"Is that right?''

"Yes. Richard wasn't married then. He was between his third and fourth wives, if memory serves me correctly.''

"I'm sure that it does.''

"Anyway, we sort of got well acquainted rather quickly. The governor acts dignified, but he's really a coldhearted lout. When someone told him that my past could hurt his future, he turned his back on me like I had a plague. I managed to extort a thousand dollars from him, enough to keep me going for a year. The man squealed like a pig and even threatened my life. That's the main reason I changed my name.''

Longarm frowned. "Why don't you look for someone with a good and honest heart?''

Diana took a drink, closing her eyes and brushing back her wet, storm-tossed hair. "Good question, and one I've asked myself about a million times.''

"And no answer?''

"Oh, yes, I know the answer, but I don't want to accept it. The fact is, Marshal, that I'm a fool and hopelessly attracted to rich and powerful men. And if they can't be either of those things, they have to be real handsome. I just can't settle for the solid farmer, the butcher, or the baker. They bore me to tears. I'd just cheat on them the way Richard has cheated on all his wives.''

Longarm didn't understand. Diana Frank seemed intent on destroying herself, even when she understood her weakness and therefore her cure.

"I know," she said. "I'm pathetic."

"I wouldn't say that."

"Well, no matter." She drank a little more quickly. "Anyway, I'll bet you haven't a boring bone in your whole big body, Marshal Long."

"Actually," he said, glancing past her to see the fading lights of Denver through the rain-streaked windows, "I spend a lot of my life doing boring things. Sometimes, though, things do get exciting when I'm somewhere tracking a man down."

She leaned forward. "Is it the hunt and then the kill that you find so exciting?"

"No, it's the challenge of trying to outguess and outwit a fugitive from the law." Longarm considered the matter carefully. "Diana, I've never really thought about it much, but I'd say the most challenging part is trying to outguess and then capture an outlaw rather than just kill him that makes it such a challenge."

"Have you 'outguessed' me?" Diana asked.

"Why should I? You're not the fugitive."

She came over to stand before him, chest pushed out, eyes bold. "Has it ever occurred to you that *I* might have been part of Nathan's plot?"

"No," he said without hesitation. "It's plain to see that you hate Nathan Cox."

Diana seemed pleased by his answer. "Well then, can you at least guess what I'm up to?"

"You want the reward money," Longarm said matter-of-factly. "Fifteen thousand dollars is enough to set yourself up for life—if you don't get messed up with another crook like Cox or spend it all foolishly."

"But I like to be foolish," she said, placing her hands on his chest and rubbing the nipples through the fabric of his shirt. "Wild, foolish, and wicked."

Longarm placed his glass of bourbon down on the polished mahogany bar and collected Diana in his arms. "I think you are probably as immoral as Governor Ganzel and that you have a perverse passion about collecting men."

She leaned in close and nuzzled his ear, her breath hot. "Is that your honest opinion?"

"Yep. You collect men like some women collect plates or silver spoons. You'll take a common working guy like me, but you prefer rich, powerful, or at least influential men. Politicians, probably judges, ranchers, and I'll bet you've even collected a successful preacher or two."

She laughed coarsely, and her hand encircled his waist as she pressed her hips hard against his own. "Marshal Long, you really *do* understand me."

"I understand that you collect all the wrong kinds of men for all the wrong reasons."

"Maybe that's about to change," she said a moment before she kissed him wetly.

Longarm knew it was crazy to mix business and pleasure—and he sure didn't want to be added to Diana's collection—but this woman made his senses reel and his manhood throb with desire. That being the case, he pulled her coat off and then undressed her as Diana began to moan and fumble with the buttons of his pants.

When Diana's dress and then her underclothes fell to her ankles, Longarm whispered, "Why don't we try the governor's plush velvet couch?''

"We'll like it," she murmured as Longarm's mouth found her small but firm breasts. He laved each one with his tongue until Diana's nipples were hard and round.

Diana groaned with pleasure and at last had her hands on his manhood which she began to stroke lightly. Longarm unbuckled his cartridge belt and let it and his holstered gun drop to the richly carpeted floor. The coach was swaying and his senses were reeling, but Longarm planted his feet wide and let the woman drop his pants.

"If we lose our balance and fall with our clothes draped around our ankles, we'll both break our necks," Diana giggled.

Longarm was of the same opinion. He pulled back and sat down heavily on the couch, tearing off his boots, pants, and underclothes.

"My, my!" Diana said, staring at his thick and stiff manhood even as she kicked off the last traces of her underclothing and fell back on the opposite couch. "I think we are going to have a *real* fun trip to Cheyenne."

"Too bad it isn't farther," Longarm said as he rushed across the coach and eagerly mounted the woman.

Diana giggled and wrapped her long, lovely legs around his back. Her pretty face assumed a dreamy expression as she closed her eyes and then bit her lower lip before saying, "Please, don't start humping me yet."

Longarm, who had already enjoyed giving the woman several strong thrusts, paused and said, "What?"

"Just let the rocking of the train drive us both slowly insane," she explained. "Marshal, I swear that is the most heavenly way."

"It could take an hour."

She opened her green eyes and stroked his bare buttocks. "We've got plenty of time, lawman, so just hold your fire. Please?"

"I'll try, but no promises."

And right about then, either the train started going over some rough track or Longarm started imagining sensations, because what happened over the next hour was like the slow buildup and then the eruption of twin volcanos. Still far, far south of the Wyoming border, both Longarm and Diana lost control and began to thrust about wildly until their juices flowed like hot lava and they roared back at the storm, clutching and slamming against each other until they slipped off the governor's couch and sprawled on the deep carpet.

"What did I tell you?" she said, kissing his face.

"You perfected this with Governor Ganzel?"

"Uh-huh. Correction. I only *thought* we had perfected it until now."

"It was good, huh?"

"Oh, yes," Diana sighed. "And the best part is that we still have hours and hours before reaching Cheyenne."

Longarm heard a huge clap of lightning and the roll of prairie thunder. "Diana, up in the locomotive, some poor engineer and coal tender are freezing and trying to stay dry. But back here we're living out a fantasy. All the good liquor we want, two soft velvet couches to mess up a little . . . and each other."

"The last part is the best part," she said, tracing a puckered scar on his left shoulder. "What happened here?"

"Bullet." He climbed off her and she stood up too, tall, slender, and desirable.

41

"And here," she said, tracing a nasty scar across his ribs.

"Knife fight."

"What about down here," Diana said, her eyes lowering to his stiff, tumescent manhood which she took in her hands. "Any scars?"

"I don't know," he said with amusement. "It's hard used and worn some, but can't remember any wounds."

"I'd better check and see for sure," Diana told him as she dropped down to her knees.

Longarm sighed and stroked her lovely hair. "Honey," he said, "you can just check it out all you like."

Diana giggled. "I'm a wicked, wicked girl, remember? And I *do* like."

Longarm closed his eyes and let her enjoy herself all she wanted.

Chapter 4

It was dark and still pouring rain when Longarm and Diana Frank reached Cheyenne and ducked into the train station, where they were immediately surrounded by four federal agents, none of whom Longarm recognized.

"Who is she?" a tall, grim-faced man in his fifties demanded to know.

"Who are *you*?" Longarm shot back.

The man's eyes flashed with annoyance. He glanced at his three grim companions and then back to Longarm before dragging out his badge. "I'm Federal Treasury Agent Supervisor Vincent Blake. These men are my agents—Matthews, Pollack, and Jones. We have identification. . . ."

"Not necessary," Longarm said, waving the offer aside. "As you have correctly guessed, I'm Deputy Marshal Custis Long, and this is my friend, Miss Diana Frank."

43

The four feds gave Diana better than a good looking over, and then Blake said, "We weren't expecting you to bring company. Nobody said anything about a woman."

"That's rather surprising," Diana said acidly. "I would have imagined that the telegraph lines between Denver and Cheyenne would have been fairly buzzing with juicy gossip."

"All the telegraph lines in and out of Cheyenne are out of commission," Blake said. "Downed by lightning."

"Well," Longarm said, shaking the rain from his Stetson, "what do you boys want?"

"I'm in charge of the investigation," Blake said. "We arrived from Washington, D.C., this morning. We have a coach waiting to take you to the hotel, where we can discuss this . . . mess in some detail."

"That'll be fine," Longarm said. "I hope that you people are paying the freight. Things happened so fast that I didn't have time to draw any travel money out of our Denver office."

"You expect *us* to pay for your room?" Jones, a sour-looking man, asked.

"Sure," Longarm said, not appreciating the combative attitude of these well-fed federal paper-pushers. "Also our food and whatever other expenses we need paid."

Jones blanched. "Well, the hell with—"

"Fair enough," Blake said, cutting off his man's protest. "We'll pay everything until you can get money sent up from Denver or we decide your information and involvement in this case is worthless."

"Worthless!" Diana snapped. "Why, I doubt that you

even know what Nathan looks like! Don't talk like such an ass, Mr. Blake. You *desperately* need us.''

The man's cheeks reddened. "We'll find out about that real soon. Let's go."

They took a carriage straight to Drover's Hotel, one of Cheyenne's finest, and not a word was spoken in the cold, wet silence. There was confusion at the check-in desk because the desk clerk had booked Longarm's room for one, not two people.

"We'll share the bed," Longarm said, appreciating the envy in the younger agent's eyes.

Diana slipped her arm through his. "Yes," she said, grinning brilliantly at the feds, "in fact, we would prefer to go to bed right now and have our little group discussion tomorrow morning. I'm feeling . . . well, rather exhausted."

"Sorry about that," Blake said, "but time is of the essence. We've got big trouble."

"The lady said she was tired," Longarm told them, his voice hardening. "I'll have a few words with you after we're comfortably settled, but—"

"Gawdammit!" Blake exclaimed. "We haven't got time to coddle you—or her!"

The muscles in Longarm's jaws corded. It took some effort to turn to the hotel desk clerk and say, "Room key, please."

"Number fourteen, Marshal Long," the clerk said. "Haven't seen you in here in about a year now."

"Our budget has been a little tight," Longarm said, "but these federal boys seem to have plenty of expense money. So send up some food. Roast turkey, steak . . . I don't care. A bottle of whiskey and—"

"Now, wait just a damn minute!" Blake protested.

"Don't you think that you've pushed your luck just about far enough already?"

"No," Longarm said as the four federal agents confronted him. "I don't think so at all. In fact, I've taken an immediate dislike to all four of you, and you are really stretching the boundaries of my civility. Now, if you'll excuse me?"

Blake was livid. But, to his credit, he maintained his composure and managed to say, "The very minute you get the lady settled, please do your damnedest to join us in the hotel bar, Marshal Long."

"I'll eat first," Longarm said, almost starting to enjoy himself. He glanced over at the hotel desk and added with a wink, "On second thought, I once had roast pheasant under glass and some excellent white wine and—"

"We will take care of it," the clerk said, returning the wink. "Thank you, gentlemen."

"You sonofabitch," Agent Jones hissed. "You're *really* asking for it."

Longarm smiled. "Didn't he say that your name was Jones?"

"That's right."

"If you keep pushing me, Jones, you'll need to wear a bib and a tag so that you can still remember your own name. Catch my meaning?"

Jones was a big man, but not as big as Longarm, and now that his bluff had been called, he folded, nodding and backing away a little. "It's just that—"

"Shut up," Longarm told the Washington agent. "Don't say any more."

"Yes, sir."

Blake snorted with anger and disgust, then spun on

his heel and marched off toward the saloon bar with his three embarrassed agents in tow.

"No traveling bags?" a bellman asked.

"Just my saddlebags and the lady's small valise," Longarm said, handing them over to the man who led them toward their room.

As soon as they were alone again, Longarm and Diana tore off their wet, rumpled clothes and jumped into bed to make love. This time they did not hold back, but quickly brought each other to a lusty climax that left them both limp and gasping.

"Boy," Diana said, grinning happily as she rolled over on top of Longarm, "you sure handled that stuffed-shirt Blake and his grouchy friends!"

"I never have liked the Washington boys," Longarm admitted. "When they come to the West, as they do on occasion, I try to avoid them. We mix like oil and water."

"Screw 'em all," Diana said. "Who needs them?"

"I could use their expense money," Longarm said. "But other than that . . . you're right. Still, I'm expected to cooperate."

"Tonight," Diana said, laying her head on his bare chest, "let's just have a wonderful meal, a hot bath, and then make love for a couple of hours and fall asleep. In the morning, after a leisurely breakfast and more love-making, maybe we can get dressed and go down to see those irritating sonofabitches."

"I'd better go down and talk to them tonight," Longarm said. "But after our dinner and the bath."

"And another session of lovemaking," she added.

"All right." Longarm chuckled. "Diana, you win."

"No," she said, tracking a faint scar on his cheek with her fingernail. "*You* win."

It was nearly midnight by the time Longarm entered the hotel bar. By then the younger federal agents were all slightly drunk. Supervisor Blake had a difficult time looking serious and sober.

"All right," Longarm said, taking a seat at their table and signaling for a whiskey, "let's get down to the facts and leave the personalities out of it, okay?"

"Okay," Jones said with the utmost respect.

"Shut . . . up," Blake ordered his man.

"Well, screw you, Vincent!" Jones swore, grabbing his drink and swaying off in a huff.

"You hurt his damned feelings," Longarm said, trying very hard not to smile.

Blake scrubbed his face. "We're all just tired. We haven't had much sleep since leaving Washington three days ago."

"Then why don't we postpone this meeting until tomorrow morning?"

"No!" Blake lowered his voice. "So what does the woman *really* know about Nathan Cox?"

"She knows how he moves."

Blake blinked. "What did you say?"

"How he moves," Longarm repeated.

"That's bullshit!" Blake exploded, slapping his hand down on the table so hard, whiskey spilled out of their glasses.

Longarm fired up a cheroot and gazed at them through the steel-blue smoke. "Do any of you hotshots realize that Nathan Cox was once an actor?"

The surprised expressions on the federal agents' faces

told Longarm that they did not know Cox had been a thespian. "Who cares?" Pollack demanded to know.

"*You* ought to care," Longarm told them, "because Nathan Cox has the ability to create many faces. Miss Frank has told me that he is an expert in disguise and that he could even be . . . that old gentleman sitting with his distinguished friends across the room from our table."

The Washington agents all swung their heads around and stared at the obviously wealthy cattle baron or banker with his fine Stetson, tailored suit, and fancy boots.

"No way!" Matthews said. "We know that Nathan Cox is only thirty-one years old."

"I have little doubt that Cox could make himself look seventy," Longarm replied. "Miss Frank told me that he once surprised her wearing a wig and woman's dress. She said that she would have sworn he was a young lady."

"Sounds like a pervert in addition to all the rest," Blake replied contemptuously.

"Don't underestimate either the man's courage or his intelligence. I'm convinced that Nathan Cox is anything but a weakling," Longarm said. "He broke his accomplice's neck, and Miss Frank says that he's a marksman as well as a vicious fist-fighter when cornered. Don't forget, he grew up on a ranch in Arizona. He's not citified like you boys."

Blake didn't like that comment, but he let it ride. "What else can you tell us?"

"Miss Frank says that he is extremely intelligent and won't do anything stupid to make my job easier."

"*Our* job," Blake corrected. "Don't forget, we're working together on this case."

Longarm could see that this was not the time or the place to argue the point. But the truth was, he had no intention of working with these men. The only reason he'd not yet given them the slip was that he needed to learn if they had a few bits of information that might help him find Nathan Cox.

The bartender brought a bottle of whiskey and a glass for Longarm, both of which he ignored. "Blake, let's get right down to the facts."

"I'd appreciate that."

"What," Longarm asked, "have you boys learned about Cox since arriving in Cheyenne?"

Blake poured himself another whiskey, and Longarm saw that his hand trembled slightly, probably from sheer exhaustion but perhaps also from the pressure he was under to resolve this mess. "Nathan Cox *is* smart," Blake sighed. "Smart enough to buy a cattle ranch with counterfeit cash."

It was Longarm's turn to be surprised. "A *Wyoming* cattle ranch?"

"That's right. We haven't been out to visit yet, and maybe we won't given this foul weather."

"No need to, Agent Pollack said."

Blake ignored the man's comment and leaned closer, his eyes intent on Longarm. "It's our understanding that Cox bought a large, well-established ranch with his bogus hundred-dollar bills."

"How much did he pay?"

"Thirty-seven thousand dollars."

Longarm whistled. That much money would buy a very big cattle ranch in Wyoming. "Didn't the seller wonder about all that newly printed cash?"

"It wasn't newly printed," Pollack said, looking

pained. "Cox washed the money, then dirtied it and let it dry. He made those bogus hundred-dollar bills look hard used."

"He must also have used some aging chemical in the wash," Blake said miserably as he pulled a hundred-dollar bill from an envelope inside his coat pocket. "Here. This is one of the bills we recovered. I defy you to say that it looks freshly printed, much less counterfeit."

Longarm took the bill and held it up to the lamplight. It looked plenty old and well used. "I'll be damned," he muttered with amazement.

"And it just gets worse," Blake said glumly. "Apparently, Cox spent a couple of nights at the gambling tables playing big-time faro and buying hundred-dollar chips. From what we can learn, he lost more than he won, but not much."

"I see," Longarm said, understanding at once. "The winning or losing wasn't the important part to Nathan Cox. What he was doing was simply exchanging the bogus bills for the chips and then he cashed everything in and laundered the twenty-seven thousand."

"That's right," Blake said, tossing down more whiskey. "The bastard has a real talent for grand larceny as well as being a counterfeiter."

Longarm frowned. "But why would Nathan Cox buy a cattle ranch?"

"That was our first question. But when we dug a little deeper, we discovered that Cox resold the ranch just three days later. He lost six thousand dollars but took some horses and a bundle of new cash out of the bank."

"Don't tell me the rest of the story," Longarm said,

deciding he also needed a drink. "By the time the dust had settled, Nathan Cox blew out of Cheyenne with some prize horses and trunkful of laundered cash."

"You guessed it," Blake said, fists balling on the tabletop.

"And you haven't a clue as to what direction he went," Longarm said, knowing the answer to the question.

"We are pretty damn sure that he didn't go back to Denver," Matthews said when his boss failed to answer.

"Maybe he did go back to Denver," Longarm said, "figuring that's the *last* direction we'd expect him to take. In fact, that's exactly what someone as bold and clever as Nathan Cox would do."

Blake's hair was thin and graying, and there were dark circles under his eyes. "You might have something there. One thing's for sure, he isn't in Cheyenne. We've spent all afternoon putting out feelers. Nothing. And with the telegraph lines down, we're sitting here blind. Frankly, we don't know which direction to turn."

"Turn south," Longarm said. "Get on the governor's train and go back down to the Denver federal building. That's where you should start."

"Are you trying to get rid of us?" Blake asked.

"No," Longarm said. "I just think Nathan Cox is smart enough to outsmart himself."

Pollack leaned close. "He might just have something, Mr. Blake. That sounds like the kind of thing Nathan Cox just might do."

"I'll think about it," Blake said, unwilling to make a commitment. "I just . . . just need a little time."

"We don't have any time," Longarm said. "The governor's train is refueling and taking on water. It will be pulling out within the hour.''

Blake sighed. ''You *are* trying to shake us.''

''No,'' Longarm said. ''I'm trying to cover a very real possibility that Blake took his laundered cash, made a disguise, and then backtracked into Colorado. From there he could go most anywhere, and my guess would be Santa Fe or Albuquerque. Though he'd have a wide-open field to play in if he headed off to New Orleans or chose to ramble around Texas.''

''Or maybe he even went to Mexico,'' Matthews said.

''A distinct possibility,'' Longarm agreed.

''All right, all right!'' Blake clasped his hands together. ''We'll take the special train back to Denver and see if we can pick up any evidence that Cox doubled back to Colorado.''

''Now you're talking,'' Longarm said. ''And when you get to the federal building tomorrow, tell Billy Vail to wire up some expense money. Until then, I'll need to borrow some cash.''

''How much?''

''Might take a couple of hundred.''

''Jaysus!'' Blake exclaimed.

Longarm shrugged innocently. ''Supervisor Blake, I have contacts here that I'll need to pay for information.''

''Damn,'' Blake muttered as he reached into his pocket for the cash.

''You going to give me the counterfeit money, or—''

''Don't even ask,'' Blake growled.

Longarm took the man's money. ''Cheer up,'' he said. ''I've been working in and through Cheyenne for years, and I know who to talk to and who to believe. First thing tomorrow morning, I'll be out on the streets, seeing if I can get some leads.''

"What about the woman?" Pollack asked, trying hard to sound matter-of-fact. "Does she need a ride back down to Denver with us in that fancy coach?"

"Don't you wish she did," Longarm said. "Sorry, but she's staying with me. After all, she's the one who can spot Cox, even in a crowd or when disguised. She's my eyes and my ears. Where I go, she goes."

"How nice for you," Pollack said sarcastically. "Sounds like you just have the world by the balls with us paying your first-class freight."

"Life never is fair," Longarm deadpanned as he came to his feet.

"So, that's it?" Blake asked, looking a little dazed with the way this meeting had gone.

"Yep," Longarm said, yawning. "I'm dog tired. You know, I was supposed to be vacationing in Boston."

"Boston ain't shit," Pollack snapped. "Bunch of people walking around like they got rods up their asses."

Longarm was amused. "You're a real funny guy, Pollack. Almost as entertaining as Jones."

"Go to hell," Pollack growled, picking up his drink and leaving.

"So when will you let us know what you learn from your informants?" Blake demanded. "I've got to answer to people back east."

"Not for a while you don't," Longarm said, "at least not until the telegraph lines are up again. And, with any luck, by then we'll have arrested Cox and this whole counterfeit thing will be history."

"You know that isn't going to happen," Blake said. "Nathan Cox might be a hundred miles from Cheyenne. Maybe a thousand if he took the last train heading for Sacramento or St. Louis."

"Or back to Denver and then on to Texas or New Mexico," Longarm drawled. "But either way, we'll find him."

Blake shook his head and struggled to his feet. "Marshal Long, I've got a sick feeling that given the company you're keeping, you aren't even in any hurry to see this case solved."

Longarm knew Supervisor Blake was referring to Diana, and he had to laugh outright.

"What's so damned funny?" Blake snarled.

"Only that you're about half right," Longarm said as he headed up to his fancy hotel room and Diana in his soft, silky bed.

Chapter 5

"I'll never understand how you got all those feds to leave us in peace and run down to Denver," Diana said the next morning as they enjoyed a leisurely breakfast in the hotel's elegant dining room.

Longarm sipped his third cup of coffee. "It wasn't hard. I just I told them that as smart as Nathan Cox is, he might just have backtracked into Colorado."

Diana thought about that a moment, and said, "Nathan really might have."

"I know. And nothing would please me more than for Agent Blake and his cronies to capture our fugitive down south. Until then, however, I need to start digging for some information right here in Cheyenne."

"Where do you start?"

"With the local marshal. He's an old friend, and he'll help if he can."

"Then let's go," Diana said, coming to her feet.

"Whoa," Longarm said. "Why don't you just go up-stairs and enjoy that wonderful hotel suite that the government is providing? After I nose around . . ."

"Oh, no," she said, quite definite about her feelings. "I've got another seventy-five hundred dollars riding on this manhunt that I mean to collect. So, don't try to get rid of me, because I'm jolly well coming with you, Marshal."

Longarm really didn't want her to come with him, but there seemed to be little choice. Besides that, Diana was smart enough to keep her mouth shut, and she might even pick up on some piece of information that he, not knowing Cox, would overlook.

"All right," Longarm said. "Let's go. First stop is the local constable's office."

"If he's as big and handsome as you," Diana said mischievously, "I'm going to enjoy this."

"Sorry, but Marshal Jeb Huff is short, overweight, and chubby," Longarm said. "He is also tough when he has to be and cool under fire. Jeb is very happily married with . . . the last I heard, four boys."

"Sounds exciting," Diana said, the tone of her voice contradicting her words.

"Jeb knows about everything that goes on in Cheyenne," Longarm assured the woman. "And what he doesn't know, he'll find out."

They left the dining room, Diana saying, "But wouldn't Marshal Huff already have told those feds everything he knew about Nathan?"

"Nope, he doesn't like easterners coming in and trying to take control any more than I would if I were in his position. In fact, he'd like nothing better than to ap-

prehend Cox without Blake's help or even his knowledge.''

"You sound like you know the marshal pretty well,''
Diana said as they headed down the street at a brisk
pace.

"Just as important, I know his breed,'' Longarm said.
"A western lawman is about as independent a fella as
you'll ever find. He's usually beholden to the city coun-
cil or a bunch of local officials for his job, but he rarely
knuckles under to them.''

"So he'd rather get fired than compromise his prin-
ciples?''

"That's right. But if he's good, and honest, he can
get a job in any of a hundred frontier towns.''

"I see.''

"Here we go,'' Longarm said as they came to a halt
before the marshal's door. "I just hope he's in and not
off chasing an outlaw or some petty thief.''

The marshal was leaning way back in his office chair,
reading a newspaper that looked as if it had be used in
the cat box. When he saw Longarm, he dropped his feet
to the rough plank floor with a bang, the forgotten paper
spilling aside.

"Well, bless my stars!'' Huff exclaimed, rushing
across the room with his hand outstretched. "If it ain't
my favorite United States deputy marshal!''

Huff cast an admiring glance at Diana, then looked
back at Longarm and exclaimed, "What did you do,
Custis, go and get married and bring the missus in to be
introduced?''

"Afraid not,'' Longarm said, blushing a little. "This
is Miss Diana Frank. She's working with me on this
Nathan Cox case.''

Huff's smile dissolved. "Ah, yes, they were here for about an hour yesterday, and, frankly, I almost decided to go fishing today so that I wouldn't have to be bothered with 'em again. Trouble is, fishin' is terrible lately.'"

Longarm grabbed a swivel chair and pushed it over to Diana. He sat down on an empty desk covered with old newspapers, dime novels, and even a few Wanted posters. "This Cox business is pretty important, Jeb."

"So I gather," the marshal replied.

"What could you tell them about our counterfeiter?"

Jeb threw up his hands. "Custis, I told them everything I knew about Cox. About his gambling and that cattle ranch he bought and then turned right around and sold for a loss."

"Who's out the big money on that one?"

"Beats me," Jeb said. "My guess is that would be the original owner, Emmett Zolliver."

"That's tough," Longarm said, shaking his head.

"You don't know the half of it," Jeb told them. "Emmett swears that he's going to keep his money, bogus or not. The guy who bought the ranch from Nathan Cox has been sick to his stomach since learning he'd been tricked. It's going to be a mess and it'll all be settled in court. I believe that our federal government bears the lion's share of the responsibility and that they'll be sued."

"I expect so," Longarm agreed. "Why don't you tell us the whole story right from the beginning. I got the gist of it last night in the hotel saloon, but the feds were half loaded and I know that there must have been things they forgot or didn't want to tell me."

"Sure," Huff said, scratching his considerable belly. "But wouldn't you and the lady rather go over to the café so that we can discuss this over coffee and some cinnamon rolls?''

"No," Longarm said, "this is something we need to keep under wraps, and I'd rather talk about it right here in the privacy of your office."

"Okay, I'll send out for the coffee and rolls," Huff said, leaving his office for a minute and signaling a boy in the street and then sending him off to get the refreshments.

"How is your wife and the kids?" Diana asked.

"They're just fine, Miss Frank. Nice of you to ask. Mind if I ask you a question?"

"Nope."

"What's your part in this Cox thing?"

"I was supposed to marry the sonofabitch," Diana said. "Instead, Nathan cleaned out my savings and took off with—"

"Cox," Longarm interrupted, "fleeced Miss Frank, but it was nothing compared to what he's doing to the government."

"How'd he get so much counterfeit money?" Jeb asked.

"Agent Blake didn't tell you?"

"His kind never does," Huff said. "That's why I don't tell *them* much of anything. But you're going to level with me, aren't you, Custis."

Longarm liked and trusted this man enough to tell him what had happened in Denver. When the story was over, Huff just shook his head. "No wonder those federal agents were in such a lather! This could really turn out big, couldn't it?"

"That's right. Now that I've leveled with you, why don't you tell us everything, especially what you didn't tell Agent Blake and his happy friends.''

Jeb Huff went over everything, and it was pretty much as Longarm had heard from Blake and his friends in the saloon the night before. He heard again how Cox had laundered the counterfeit money and bought as well as sold a big cattle ranch.

''Which ranch was it?'' Longarm asked.

''The Bar Z. Homesteaded sixty years ago by Emmett. Everyone expected him to leave it to his two sons, Clyde and Buck, but I knew that Emmett was too wise a man to do that. Those boys aren't worth the powder it would take to blow their noses off. They're trigger-happy troublemakers and have already set off after Nathan Cox. And if they find Cox, there's little doubt that they'll torture him to death and steal everything he's got including the bogus money, which they'll spend like a pair of drunken sailors in a foreign port of call.''

''Any idea where they went?'' Longarm asked.

''They got drunk the night before they left and told everyone in the saloon that Cox had run southwest toward the Wasatch Mountains of Utah.''

''Big, rugged mountains,'' Longarm said. ''I've been in them a time or two. They could even get snow this early.''

''Damn right they can,'' Jeb agreed. ''If Buck, Clyde, and that counterfeiter get snowed under in those mountains, you might never find any of them.''

''Did they say *how* they knew that Nathan was heading in that direction?'' Diana asked.

''No,'' Huff said. ''But I expect that someone reported seeing him and those blooded horses hightailing it that way. Custis might want to talk to the boys' father.

61

Old Emmett is in town, and lately he's been pretty drunk most of the time.''

"He sounds difficult," Longarm said.

"He's meaner than a teased snake," Jeb admitted. "But you might find a way to get him to talk if he understands that you want Nathan Cox as bad as he does."

"Where can I find Emmett?"

"Probably drinking in the Maverick."

"I know the place well," Longarm said. "It's got quite a reputation."

"That's right. I sure wouldn't take a woman in there," Jeb said. "The Maverick is rough."

"I'm a lawman, remember?"

Jeb blinked and then looked embarrassed. "Yeah, Custis, for a moment I forgot that I am too. Let's just go. The coffee and rolls can wait until we get back."

Longarm glanced at Diana, who said, "With *two* lawmen to protect me, why should I be worried?"

"No reason," Longarm said. "No reason at all."

Cigarette and cigar smoke wafted over the swinging doors to the Maverick. Longarm could hear the arguing and cussing a good fifty strides before they entered the place. The Maverick was where Cheyenne's worst element went to drink, gamble, and use women in the cribs tucked away back in the saloon's former storerooms. Shootings and knifings were a common occurrence there, and for as long as Custis could recall, the saloon was the kind of place where men entered at their own peril.

"I pass through this shit-house once a day," Jeb said, sounding apologetic. "But the minute I'm gone, things go to bad again."

"Why don't you just shut the place down?"

"Don't think I haven't thought about doing that for years," Jeb said. "But every town has a place where the worst element goes. It keeps them separated from the decent people. If I shut this saloon down, the criminal element would spill over and there'd be more killing of the innocent. Besides that, the saloon pays a penalty to the city, which needs their money."

"Makes no sense to me," Longarm said, "but Cheyenne is your town."

"Yep," Jeb said. "And I like to keep the rotten apples in the same dirty barrel. Miss Frank, I really—"

"I can handle this," she said, cutting him off. "I've worked in some rough saloons."

They went inside and all heads turned. One huge, bearded man, upon seeing Diana, guffawed and came hollering and striding across the room. Longarm wasn't sure of the giant's intentions, so he just drew his gun and pistol-whipped the man before he could do any damage.

"Hey!" one of the patrons exclaimed. "You can't just walk in here and do that to Ernie!"

"Sure he can," Marshal Huff shouted. "And if you don't mind your own business, the same will happen to you. Emmett! We need to talk."

The rancher twisted around, his eyes bloodshot and his face stubbled with a gray beard. "Got nothin' to say to you, Jeb. Not a single gawddamn word."

"Damn," Longarm muttered, "why don't I ever come across an easy one."

"Let me handle him," Diana said, surprising everyone by marching across the room and sidling up to the rancher.

Emmett Zolliver wasn't a big or physically imposing

63

man anymore, but he had been before the years, the hard Wyoming weather, and the whiskey had all combined to take their toll on his once-powerful body. Now he glared at Diana, probably expecting her to cringe, but she didn't.

"Mind if I have a drink?" she asked, her eyes darting to his bottle.

"You want to drink this panther piss?"

"Sure! It says on the bottle that it's whiskey."

He squinted at her, and when she met his eyes without flinching, he grabbed his half-empty bottle by the neck and upended it, gulping several big slugs.

"You want to drink, do it," he challenged Diana, shoving the bottle in her direction.

"Oh, kee-rist," Jeb whispered, starting forward.

But Longarm grabbed his arm. "Hold up, she knows what she's doing."

The whole saloon was staring as Diana wrenched the bottle from the embittered old man, upended it, then drank its entire contents. Longarm saw her shudder a little, but then she smiled and slammed the bottle down on the bar and demanded, "Now, why don't you tell me where the hell I can find Nathan Cox!"

Everyone, even Emmett Zolliver, grinned after they'd recovered from shock. Longarm went over to join them and heard the old man say, "Well now, miss, you *are* my kind of woman. Bartender, bring us another bottle."

Longarm guessed that Diana was going to learn about everything she wanted to know in the next few hours. The question then was whether they were going to be able to walk out of the Maverick, or would they have to be carried out.

Chapter 6

Nathan Cox had driven his half-dozen blooded Thoroughbred horses over the Laramie Mountains and then skirted around the north slope of Bridger Peak before dropping south toward the Yampa River in the northwest corner of Colorado. It had been his intention to roughly parallel the Union Pacific Railroad line, but then he'd decided that would be far too risky. No doubt, there were feds riding the rails, seeking him, that very minute.

Nathan wasn't worried. He had fast horses and plenty of cash whose serial numbers couldn't be tracked. Furthermore, he was quite sure that the pursuit would lead south into Arizona and that the federal agents would be waiting for him in the vicinity of Prescott and Flagstaff. Let them wait. The first half of his journey would be in the direction of Arizona, but then he'd veer north, cross the hard, high-desert country of central Nevada, and then follow the Sierras south a little into California, where he understood there was some prime ranching country to be had at very attractive prices.

California's eastern Sierra slope was the last place anyone in the world would expect him to run. Other than a few mining towns like Bodie, all reputed to be in serious decline, there was no reason to expect a rich fugitive to settle in that country, where there just wasn't much for a man to spend his fortune on.

The only trouble was, this was a hard, lawless land he was crossing, one known to be a stronghold of roving bands of cut-throats and cattle rustlers. And, unfortunately, three of them were heading in his direction at that very moment.

Nathan wore a two-shot .45-caliber derringer in his sleeve and a Colt .45 on his hip. In addition to that, he had a good Winchester repeating rifle in his saddle scabbard and a Bowie knife hidden in his boot top. But Nathan had little doubt that the three rough-looking men still a quarter of a mile away and trotting toward him were equally well armed and perhaps even as proficient with their weapons.

"Well," he said as he continued herding his horses, "I might be able to outrun the bunch of them. But then they'd know I was afraid and had a lot to lose and so they'd keep coming after me. Or I can just open up on them first and hope to drop one, maybe even two . . . but then the third would probably put a bullet in me before I could get around to him."

Nathan frowned. Both choices were bad, and there was the slim chance that these three riders were honest cowboys, men just coming to pass the time of day before continuing eastward. Nathan didn't want to kill decent, hardworking men. Breaking his accomplice's neck back in Denver had left a bad taste in his mouth and, if Tom hadn't decided to suddenly get greedy, he'd still be alive today.

I'll give them a chance, he thought. *Maybe they are friendly and mean me no harm.*

When there was still about three hundred yards between himself and the three riders, Nathan saw one of them reach for the pistol at his side and then ease it up and down in his holster. That convinced him that the men had deadly intentions. He took the precaution of slipping his derringer out of his right sleeve and transferring it to his left hand. Nathan had taught himself to shoot quite accurately with either hand, should he ever find himself outnumbered and in a rather desperate situation such as this might become.

"Howdy!" the man on the high-headed gray horse shouted.

"Howdy!" Nathan called in return, spurring his mount forward so that he would meet this trio in advance of his band of fine horses.

When Nathan was out in front, he drew in his reins, cocked his derringer, and kept it folded under his fingers and behind the horn of his saddle. The three men also reined up, and the man on the gray thumbed back his droopy hat.

"Nice horses, mister."

"Thanks."

"Where you heading?"

"South."

"Where you come from?" an angular, greasy-haired man with evil-looking eyes on a buckskin wanted to know.

"Rock Springs."

Nathan took a quick glance at the third and youngest outlaw. Probably not out of his teens, the kid looked damned worried. He wore baggy clothes and clodhopper boots, the kind that farmers and homesteaders favored. Nathan didn't miss the fact that there was a gun strapped around his thin waist and reminded himself that he could not afford to overlook the kid, who was probably as deadly as a baby rattlesnake. Even so, the kid would be the third target, while the man on the gray would be the first and the bad-eyed one would earn Nathan's second bullet.

The man on the gray horse dropped his gun hand to his side and eased up a little in his stirrups. He surveyed Nathan's band of exceptional horses and smiled. "Well now, stranger, do you have a bill of sale for those horses?"

"I do," Nathan said, feeling his heart begin to pound. "But why do you ask?"

"Been a lot of horse stealing up around Rock Springs," the leader said with a cold, almost mocking grin. "And you are a stranger to these parts."

"I'm just passing through, mister. Looking to go to Arizona, where the winters are warm."

"Yeah," the thin man said. "But what if you *stole* them horses? And what if we didn't ask to see your bill of sale? Why, we'd be plumb negligent, wouldn't we, Brady?"

"We would for a fact," the man on the gray said. "And I *hate* to be negligent. What do you say, kid?"

The kid took a deep breath and managed to nod his head. Nathan noticed how his hand also inched toward the butt of the six-gun that seemed too large for his body.

"Kid don't talk much," Brady explained. "But I'm

sure the kid is as eager to see that bill of sale as we are.''

Nathan knew their game. They'd expect him to bury his right hand in his pocket or his saddlebags and that's when they'd draw and shoot him off his horse. They'd probably done it more than once and, when bracing the foolish or unwary, it posed little risk.

''You want to see my bill of sale right now?'' he asked, pretending to be a little slow even as his mind ticked off the sequences that he would go through in order to kill these three men and survive.

''That's right,'' the thin one said, his lips drawing back with contempt. ''Let's see your gawddamn bill of sale! We ain't got all damned day.''

Act as if they're scaring you shitless, Nathan reminded himself. *Let them feel overconfident so they relax just a hair and then kill the first two with your derringer.*

Nathan looped his reins over his saddle horn and absently patted his coat pocket as if he were starting to search for the bill of sale. At the same time, he nudged his mount ever so lightly with the heels of his boots so that it stepped even closer to his enemies. Close enough to almost reach out and touch the heads of their horses because, when it came to using a derringer, closer was always better in order to plant both your bullets in their chests.

''Let me see here,'' he said, reaching his lower coat pockets and then raising his left hand as if he were going to check his shirt pocket.

''Hey!'' the thin man screamed, his hand diving for his gun. ''He's got—''

Nathan had a very sudden change of heart. The thin man was definitely his first target because he was extremely fast. But not fast enough to draw his heavy six-gun when Nathan's derringer was already up and pointed at his narrow chest. Nathan's derringer barked smoke and fire, and the man on the buckskin slapped at his heart, then stared as he began to topple forward in death.

Nathan's left hand had only to shift a couple of inches before it rested on Brady. The man was big and slow. Nathan would have taken more time to place his bullet if it had not been for the kid. As it was, when the derringer barked again, Brady took the slug just below his rib cage. The big man screamed like a panther and his eyes bugged. He tried to fire but hadn't the strength, so he grabbed at his gut, blood pumping out between his thick fingers.

Nathan's hand released the now-empty derringer. He went for his six-gun but froze when he saw that the kid already had the drop on him. For an instant they just stared at each other. The kid had every reason to pull his trigger . . . but didn't. He just held his gun out and sighted down its barrel.

"I reckon I hold your life in my hands, mister," the kid said in a voice that trembled. "I reckon I'm more important to you right now than God."

Nathan felt sweat erupt all over his body. "I reckon that's true enough," he said in a voice that didn't sound like his own.

"I ought to kill you and take the whole damn bunch of these horses. With your guns and rifles, the saddles and everything, I bet I could get five hundred dollars. Easy."

"I don't think you'd get very far," Nathan said, desperate to buy time enough to find the advantage. "You'd run into some more like those two friends of yours. This country is crawling with their kind of vermin. You wouldn't get fifty miles.''

The kid was blue-eyed with sand-colored hair and freckles. He looked as if he ought to still be in school or holding a bamboo pole beside a fishing hole instead of being in a position to be the last one standing after a gunfight.

''What's your name?''

''Nathan.''

''Did you *really* buy them fine horses?''

''I did,'' Nathan said truthfully. ''And I do have a legal bill of sale in my saddlebags to prove it.''

''What you got so heavy and resting under a tarp aboard that pack animal?''

''You mean packed on my mule?''

''He's your only pack animal. You got him loaded down real good. You got gold in that pack?''

Nathan even dared to glance around at the mule, which was, of course, carrying the Treasury Department's heavy printing plates and paper as well as his own supplies.

''No,'' Nathan said. ''They're printing plates.''

''What are you totin' them around for?''

Lies were like habits to Nathan. They came easy and without conscious thought. ''I'm an editor,'' he said. ''I'm looking for someplace to set up shop.''

The kid's brow furrowed. ''You mean to do a news-paper?''

''That's right.''

''I wish I could read,'' the kid said. ''But I never had the time to learn. Worked in my pappy's fields since damn near the time I could follow a mule and swing a hoe.''

71

"So why didn't you stick to farming?" Nathan asked, curious.

"I *hated* farmin'!" The gun shook in the kid's hand. "Farmin' killed Ma when I was six. Killed Pappy ten years later and ruined my brothers and sisters. Not one of us stayed on the homestead. All of us run off."

"You chose to run with real bad company," Nathan said, beginning to realize that the kid probably didn't want to murder him.

"Well," the kid said, gazing down at the two dead men. "They kept us in bacon and beans and the work wasn't hard."

"What was the work?"

"Nothin' big. We just 'borrowed' a lot of things."

"They were going to kill me for my horses," Nathan said. "And that would have made you a partner in murder."

"I wouldn't have been able to stop 'em," the kid said. "If I'd said anything against what they had in mind, they'd as soon as not killed me too."

Nathan drew a deep breath. "All right, so what happens now?"

"I want to see if that's really printin' stuff, or maybe it's gold."

"And if it were gold, would you kill me for it?" Nathan asked point-blank.

"I dunno," the kid said, shrugging his thin shoulders. "But I'll bet you'd kill me given half a chance."

"You're wrong," Nathan said. "Let me ride on and we both live to see tomorrow's sunrise."

The kid thought about this for almost a minute before he said, "I got no job, nothin' much I care to do either. Maybe we could work together."

"No."

The kid lowered his gun and he looked hurt. "Well . . . well, why not?"

"You can't read, what good would you do for me?"

"I can shoot and you might come across a couple more like you just killed and not be so lucky a second time."

"You think I was lucky?"

"Some," the kid said. "Some lucky, some just damned good with weapons. And as for helpin' you, I know horses. I could help take care of 'em and also back you in a fight."

"Maybe."

"Watch," the kid said, lifting the barrel of his six-gun. "You see that pine cone yonder?"

"Which one?" Nathan said, twisting around in his saddle.

"The one that I'm just about to blast to smithereens," the kid said, firing a shot that caused one of the low-hanging pine cones to explode. "Not bad, huh?"

"It was damn good," Nathan agreed, knowing now that it was a wise decision that he had not gone for his gun, because the farmer boy would have drilled him squarely through the heart. "Do you know this country?"

"Like the back of my hand. I was raised over the mountains in the Utah Territory, but we'd come up here for timber and to hunt in the fall."

"Then you'd know a pass over the Wasatch into the Great Basin?"

"I know lots of passes, but they'll be closin' up soon on account of the snow."

"I want to get over these mountains," Nathan said.

73

"If you can guide me, I'll pay you well."

The kid's eyes tightened at the corners. "I could just take everything."

"Then why haven't you already shot me?" Nathan asked.

The kid surprised him with a grin. "You're not only dangerous, you're smart, makin' you even more dangerous. All right, I believe you when you say there ain't no gold on that pack mule. And I ain't the killin' kind unless I have to be."

"You ever killed anyone?"

"Nope."

"Holster your gun," Nathan said, "and let's get out of here."

"Wouldn't we want to take their guns and such?"

"No," Nathan said.

But the kid climbed down from his horse and went over to rob the bodies. "They got at least seventy dollars each on 'em," he said, pulling cash out of their pockets. "And better guns than mine. I can't leave so much behind."

"Suit yourself," Nathan said, watching as the kid even removed the rings and cheap pocket watches from the bodies.

"Let's go," the kid said after trading boots with the thin man and then remounting his horse.

The kid jammed his gun into his holster and smiled. "You want to get over the mountains, you'd best not kill me, mister."

"All right," Nathan said, deciding he liked the simple kid. "I won't kill you."

"Not even after we get through the passes?"

"No," Nathan said, meaning it. "Not even then. I

actually could use you as insurance in case I run into more thieves, rustlers, and cutthroats.''

"I won't run out on you, mister."

"You have a real name?"

"Rolf," the kid said. "Rolf Swensen. My parents were Swedish."

"All right, Rolf Swensen. Let's put some miles between us and those dead men."

"Can we take their horses?"

"No. They might be recognized and get us into more trouble than they're worth."

"I'd be willing to take that chance," Rolf said.

Nathan's hand patted his holstered gun. "Well," he said, "I wouldn't. And since I'm going to be the one making the decisions, we leave the horses? Any problem with that, Rolf?"

"No sir," the kid said. "Just don't shoot me in the back after I get you over these mountains."

"I won't," Nathan said. "Just point us to the pass and let's go."

Rolf looked glad to do just that. Neither man so much as bothered to look back at the two corpses staring up at the cool blue sky.

Chapter 7

On their second day in the mountains, a cold rain began to fall and Nathan was smiling because their tracks would all be washed away clean.

"What the devil are you so happy actin' about?" Rolf wanted to know. "This could turn to snow up in the passes and we could get stuck and freeze to death."

"If it begins to snow, we'll backtrack and head due south toward New Mexico," Nathan decided. "We'll ride all the way down to the Colorado River and then cut west."

"Where are we going?"

Nathan was a man who did not believe in telling anyone his future plans, especially this kid. "We're going southwest," he said vaguely.

"To Arizona?"

"Yeah."

"I'd like that," Rolf said, looking a little happier. "It

will be warm and *dry* down there in the desert. "What are you going to do with these fine horses?"

"I don't exactly know," Nathan admitted. "Maybe sell 'em, maybe see if a few of them can run fast enough to win me some money."

"I'd like one of them horses," Rolf said, nodding. "My own horse ain't much, as you can plainly see. Could I have one of your horses when we get where we're goin'?"

"I expect you can," Nathan said, wondering what the kid would say if he knew that there were tens of thousands of dollars in the packs and everything necessary to counterfeit upward of a million dollars.

"Boy!" Rolf said, a wide grin splitting his hatchet-shaped face. "I'd sure be happy about that! If I had any one of them horses to ride—especially that dapple-gray gelding—I could get a *real* cowboyin' job. Or, maybe at least one doin' fence ridin'."

"Fence riding sounds pretty boring."

"Oh, no, it ain't! I'd like nothin' better than to ride fence all day on a fine horse like that dapple gray. Take my thirty dollars a month. Not have a care in the world. No sir! Just ride fence all day and watch the clouds blow around in the sky."

Nathan had never known anyone quite as simple as Rolf. He was childlike, and unless you knew better, it was easy to assume that he was mentally deficient. But Rolf knew a lot about farming and the country. He could tell you many things about the birds and animals they often saw in the distance. No, he wasn't stupid, just simple, and Nathan knew that there was a big difference.

"Wouldn't you like to *own* a ranch?" Nathan asked, having to grit his teeth to keep them from chattering.

"Nope."

"But why?"

"Too much worry for my mind," Rolf said with a decisive nod of his head. "If someone else owned it, you could have a steady job without any worry. Don't you see, Nathan?"

"I guess," Nathan said, not seeing at all. "If I buy a ranch, I'll let you ride fence for me. It'd be up to you."

Why, I'd like that a lot!"

"Well," Nathan said, "I plan to buy and sell a couple of ranches. Maybe I'll even keep the best one and you can ride its fences on that dapple horse."

Rolf looked like he'd died and gone to heaven. "I just can't think of anything nicer."

"What about girls?" Nathan asked out of curiosity. "Did you ever know a girl?"

"Why sure! I knowed lots of girls. Had four sisters. Two older, two younger. I know all about girls."

"That's not what I meant," Nathan said. "What I meant was if you ever slept with a girl?"

"Yeah," Rolf said, dipping his chin and avoiding looking over at Nathan. "I slept with my sisters every winter until I was twelve. We only had a few blankets and it was warmer that way . . . but they all snored."

Nathan actually chuckled. "I give up," he said. "I don't think you ever had a girl."

"There was one that was different than my sisters," Rolf confessed. "I wanted to kiss her, but kindly don't tell anybody."

"Oh, I wouldn't do that. What was her name?"

Rolf's face softened. "Her name was Miss Sally May-field and she was real pretty, Nathan. But she upped and got married and, for some darned reason, wouldn't hardly speak to me no more. After that I gave up on 'em.''

"Probably a hasty decision," Nathan said. "The right women can bring a lot of pleasure to a man."

Rolf's cheeks reddened. "I guess I'd better ride on up ahead," he said, spurring his sorry horse into a trot.

Nathan watched the kid ride away. He was so pathetic, he was actually kind of endearing. Like a puppy or something, only this pup had fangs. Nathan again reminded himself of how good Rolf was with a gun and how he'd better not forget the exploding pine cone.

"Whiskey Creek is just up ahead," Rolf announced near sundown as they rode through the cold and drenching rain. "But it's a rough place, so maybe we shouldn't stop."

"Have they got a saloon, a gambling hall, and a hotel with dry beds?"

"Yeah, but—"

"Then that's where we'll spend the night," Nathan said. "How much farther?"

"Right up ahead, less'n a mile."

"Anyone in Whiskey Creek know you were riding with those two men I killed?"

"I don't know. Maybe."

"Then you'll stay in the room and that way there will be no problems," Nathan said. "I'll have some food brought up."

"Be mighty nice of you," Rolf said. "Haven't slept in a hotel room much."

"No," Nathan said, "I don't expect that you have. Well, you will tonight and every other night we can find one."

"Cost a lot of money to stay in hotel rooms every night."

"It's *my* money," Nathan said, "so don't let it worry at your mind."

Lightning crashed in the distance, and when the roll of thunder passed, Rolf shouted, "But if you spend all your money on hotels, Nathan, you won't have none left to buy that ranch and I won't have a job ridin' your fences!"

Nathan just shook his head. "It'll all turn out fine, Rolf. Trust me."

"Yes, sir, but I sure wish you'd save your money. We could put up our horses and stay with 'em at the livery and save lots."

"Not on your simple life!" Nathan yelled into the storm as the lights of Whiskey Creek blurred wetly through the falling rain. "Not on your life!"

From the lights, Nathan could tell that Whiskey Creek was a decent-sized town with at least a couple of thousand residents.

"First stop is the livery," he said.

"It's at this end of town," Rolf said. "But old man Waite is kind of a sourpuss, and I doubt he'll be very happy to have us show up in a storm."

"Don't worry, I'll even make him smile," Nathan promised.

"How?"

"Cash always makes a man happy. I'll just pay him enough to keep grinning."

"You don't know Waite."

"Maybe not," Nathan agreed, "but I sure do know the power of cash."

When they arrived at the livery with their horses, it took some doing to get the old liveryman to open his barn door. He wore bib overalls, had a full beard, smelled like a pig, and constantly spat tobacco juice.

"I'm closed!" he roared at them through the rain. "Gawdammit! What are you pair of fools doing out in this nasty weather!"

"Passing through," Nathan said. "As you can see, I've got a bunch of fine horses and they need shelter. Do you have dry stalls in this barn?"

"For all them horses?" Waite asked, looking past the men to the bedraggled band.

"Yeah," Nathan said, getting angry and impatient as the rain began to fall even harder. "Can we come in and talk, or do we have to sit here in this pouring rain and haggle?"

"Before any of you come inside, you'd better know that it will cost you plenty for all those horses," Waite warned.

"I can pay a fair price."

"And for another thing," Waite said, "hay is at a premium this time of year."

"I want them all grained and curried," Nathan said, ignoring the fool. "Every last one of them."

"Then come on inside," Waite finally offered. "But leave that fool Rolf Swensen and the horses *outside* until I see the color of your money."

Nathan glanced over at the wet and bedraggled kid. "This will only take a minute."

"He's gonna skin you alive," Rolf warned.

"Maybe."

Nathan spurred his mount into the barn and dismounted. He swept off his hat, sending rainwater flying. The interior of the barn was dim and dusty. Nathan saw only two horses in the whole big place.

"You better be willing to pay me handsomely for this trouble, or you can ride on, storm or no damned storm," Waite threatened.

"What do you consider 'handsomely'?"

"Two dollars a horse per night. 'Course, that would cover the grain and the curryin'. I got a boy that comes over, but the little shit doesn't work cheap."

"Why don't *you* curry them?"

"I'm way too old and lazy. Now, mister, do you want to pay . . . or ride?"

Nathan reached into his left pocket, where he kept a roll of counterfeit hundred-dollar bills. When he pulled them out and laid them flat in the palm of his hand, Waite's watery old eyes bugged.

"Holy jaysus!" the old liveryman exclaimed. "What did you do, rob a bank?"

"No, the United States Mint."

The old man barked a laugh. "I *believe* you!"

"Here," Nathan said, giving the old man one of the bills. "You take real good care of these horses. Clean our saddles and equipment and then soak them in a good leather oil. We'll settle up the account when I am ready to leave town."

"Why . . . why sure! How long are you stayin', mister?"

"That all depends on how much I enjoy myself here. I assume that there are plenty of poker games and pretty women in this town?"

"Yes, sir! And, with all your money, you'll have both comin' to find you."

"Just don't say anything about the money, Mr. Waite. If I hear that you've been gossiping or that you've touched any of my packs, it'll cost you a big tip. You see, I'm a newspaperman and I've got some plates and stuff that I don't want tampered with. Is that understood?''

Waite couldn't keep his eyes off all the hundred-dollar bills. "Whatever you say," he said. "I mean to please."

"Ask the kid to come in," Nathan said, removing his saddlebags and then leading the pack horse with the treasury plates into the nearest stall. "And *smile* at him, Mr. Waite! Make him feel welcome!"

"Yes, sir!" the old man cried, grinning so broadly that he looked like he'd been stricken with facial rigor mortis.

"What did you ever do to make him so happy?" Rolf asked as soon as they were on their way back through the mud and rain to the best hotel in town.

"I paid him a lot more money than he expected," Nathan shouted as a particularly loud boom of thunder shook the heavens.

"Dammit, you're going to spend *all* our ranch money!" Rolf yelled as they jumped out of the street and onto the boardwalk, then marched into the hotel. "You ain't going to have enough money left to buy even an acre of sagebrush if you don't be careful."

"Maybe not," Nathan said, stomping his boots and whipping water from his Stetson as he marched across the lobby floor and planted himself in front of the solid walnut registration desk. "Clerk!"

An older gentleman appeared. He wore a suit and tie, and when he saw Nathan and Rolf, muddy and unshaven, he frowned, drummed his fingers impatiently, and said, "Yes?"

"Two rooms with baths," Nathan ordered. "Two of your *best* rooms."

The clerk studied them and then he said, "I'm afraid that our rates might be a little more than you might wish to pay."

Once again Nathan dragged out his roll of hundred-dollar bills, and although this old man was well dressed and dandified, his reaction varied little from that of the liveryman Waite. In a matter of moments Rolf and Nathan were being escorted to their rooms.

"You just paid him a hundred dollars?" Rolf whispered when they were back in his room.

"Yes, but look at all the service we're getting!"

"Yeah," Rolf said. "I never even dreamed that I'd stay in a place nearly so nice."

"Well," Nathan promised, "just stick around, because things are even going to get better."

"What do you mean?"

"I mean food, wine, and women," Nathan said. Earlier, he had asked the old desk clerk, who'd turned out to be an exceptionally accommodating fellow, "Mister, where can I find pretty women to share our supper and company?"

The old gentleman acted offended. "We have only two kinds of females in Whiskey Creek. Ladies and . . . and whores."

"I want two whores," Nathan said happily. "The best that money can buy in this town. Send for them right now."

"I can't do that! Please, sir! This is a *respectable* establishment!"

"Here," Nathan said, peeling off another hundred-dollar bill. "You just find us some respectable-looking girls and do this anyway you want. Pay them fairly and keep the change, but serve them up with our dinner. If

I'm happy, you're going to be *very* happy when we check out in a few days. Understand?''

The old man showed every last one of his teeth—even the molars—as he folded the bill and hurried away.

"It's going to get better real soon, Rolf. Real soon."

"What. . . .''

"Take a bath and come over when dinner and the girls arrive," Nathan told his young friend. ''Shave and put on something that smells good.''

"I lost my shaver and—''

"We'll provide those," a young hotel clerk said, appearing like magic.

"Excellent," Nathan said, tipping the boy with a twenty-dollar bill. "And use that to find us both some clean, dry clothes. Things serviceable for the trail, but with a little style. Do you understand?''

"Perfectly," the young man assured him. "But the stores are probably closed, sir.''

"Here," Nathan said, giving the young man another twenty. "Besides the clothes, bring us whiskey—no, champagne. The most expensive cigars in town and . . . well, I'll think of other things as the evening progresses. Right now, of course, we need our bathtubs filled!''

"Yes, sir!''

The next several hours were like a dream to Rolf. He took a long, hot bath and was embarrassed at how muddy the water became because of the grime on his body and in his hair. Afterward, Rolf shaved his cheeks and the little stubble on his chin with a fine, sharp razor, then doused himself from head to toe with cologne and tried on a new set of clothes. Just before going next door to Nathan's room, he even combed his hair, parting it neatly in the middle.

"If only you could see me now, Mother," he whispered just before going out to knock on Nathan's door.

"It's unlocked!" Nathan shouted. "Come on in, Rolf! You're holding up our party!"

When Rolf opened the door, he saw Nathan and two pretty women sitting on the bed. Before them rested a large silver cart with a silver tray loaded with steaming potatoes, steaks, and all manner of wonderful-smelling food.

"Hungry?" Nathan asked with a wink.

"Like a winter-starved wolf."

The younger of the girls was no more than Nathan's age. She wasn't as pretty as the woman that had her arm around Nathan's waist, but she was plenty nice with long red hair and she was slender, the way that Sally had been before she started having children. She had a pointed chin and big robin's-egg-blue eyes.

"Hello," she said sweetly as she came up to stand before Rolf. "I'm going to enjoy becoming . . . friends."

Rolf gulped. "We're going to become friends?"

"That's right. Nathan has told me all about you. You're much handsomer than I'd expected, and I know that you are very brave." Her fingertips brushed Rolf's stinging cheeks and sent shivers racing up and down his spine. "Are you really, really hungry?"

"I'm starved, actually."

"Good! My name is Teresa and I'm starved too. Let's go eat first."

Rolf hadn't the slightest idea what the "first" part meant. But he could smell the food, even over all the stinkwater that he'd doused himself with. Pushing past

Teresa, he went to gobble up his share.

"Rolf, slow down and quit stuffing your face. And you gotta go a little easier on cologne," Nathan said, waving at the air and making a face. "You're just a little overpowering."

Rolf's feelings were hurt. "I'm sorry, sir. Maybe I should leave."

"Hell no! But after you've had your fill of eating, let Teresa give you a bath and wash some of that cologne off."

Rolf blushed and he felt like Teresa must also be withering with shame. "Besides," he managed to say, "I just had a hot bath!"

"Have another," Nathan said, stuffing a cube of steak into his mouth and sipping at his good whiskey. "Teresa, call the hotel desk and have them make another bath for Rolf!"

"Whatever you say!"

Rolf enjoyed his food so much, he forgot that his feelings were supposed to be hurt. And as soon as he was stuffed, Teresa took his hand and they went back to his room, where a second clear, steaming bath waited.

"It's new, clean water all right," Rolf said, testing it.

"Of course it is," Teresa said sweetly as she began to unbutton his new shirt.

"What are you doing?" Rolf said, although he was beginning to think he knew what she was doing.

"We're going to take a bath together," Teresa said, a big smile on her face.

Rolf felt his blood begin to surge in his ears and his tongue went thick and stuck so that he had to work up a little spittle in order to speak. "Together?"

"Sure. Didn't you ever take a bath with your sisters?"

"Yeah, when I was little."

"Well, it won't be so different now."

"Teresa, I think it will be."

She smiled patiently. "Rolf, let's just pretend that we're little children again. Okay? I'm sure that will make you feel comfortable."

Rolf wasn't sure, but he didn't want to upset Teresa, so he nodded, and, quick as a flash, she had his clothes off and then her own and they were slipping into the warm, soapy water.

"Big tub," he managed to say, deathly afraid to touch her even with his toes.

"It's just the right size," Teresa said, leaning forward and then tipping right over on top of him.

"Hey!" he cried, struggling to keep from slipping underwater. "My sisters didn't come over to my end of the tub!"

"I know," she said, finding his already rising manhood and encircling it with expert fingers. "But we're going to be *friends,* remember?"

"I never had no friend do this either," he gasped as her hand began to do things to his worm that made his toes tingle.

"Relax," Teresa whispered, everything is coming along right on schedule. "We're going to have a real good time and play lots of games tonight."

"Oh . . ." he heard himself say in a voice too high to be his own. "I'm not very good at games."

"I'm going teach you all you need to know, honey."

Rolf felt her legs spread and then his worm somehow got poked up inside of her and got much, much warmer. Teresa sighed and giggled in his ear as her bottom began to make little waves.

"Rolf, how do you like *this* game?"

"I never liked anything better in my whole life," he panted, placing his hands on her back and them sliding them down to Teresa's buttocks. "And you're softer than anything I ever touched. Softer even than a furry little kitten."

Teresa began to make a purring sound as her bottom moved around and around under the water, causing some to lap over the sides of the tub and soak the floor.

Rolf didn't much give a damn. He closed his eyes and hoped he could die, because he knew that nothing ever again would feel so good. No matter what, there would never be anything nicer to remember than this bath with Teresa, but he was mighty, mighty glad that his dear mother couldn't see him now.

Chapter 8

Longarm had a hangover the next morning when he slogged through the mud and pouring rain to reach the telegraph office in downtown Cheyenne.

"Whew!" the telegraph operator exclaimed as thunder crashed somewhere out on the prairie. "Marshal Long, ain't this storm a sonofabitch though! I never saw so much rain!"

"It's pretty awful all right," Longarm agreed, stomping his boots and shaking water off himself. "John, how are the wife and all your kids?"

"They're fine. Everyone is hoping that this rain don't turn to sleet. Kinda early in the year to be putting up with this cold weather."

"Yes, it is," Longarm said. "And it looks like I'm going to have to start a manhunt."

"I suspect that you'd be going after that counterfeiter."

John Fosdick was a genial man in his early forties who liked to wear bow ties and smoke the rankest-smelling cigars money could buy. Longarm had spent quite a few enjoyable hours with the telegraph operator either sending or waiting to receive messages to and from his Denver office. Fosdick yearned to be a lawman and talked endlessly about outlaws and gunfighters. The man even kept a journal of all the Wanted posters that Marshal Huff kept in his office. Longarm knew that the telegraph operator's dream was to capture a killer and collect the reward, but not so much for the money itself. He longed for the fame and satisfaction.

"Did you meet Nathan Cox?" Longarm asked the man.

"Yep," Fosdick said. "He waltzed right in here and sent a couple of telegrams the day before he vanished."

Longarm's interest picked up. "Do you happen to remember who he sent the telegrams to?"

Fosdick began to doodle on a pad of paper. "Marshal, you know that Western Union has a policy against giving out that information."

"I need to know," Longarm said, emptying his shirt pocket of cheroots and laying them neatly on the counter between them.

Fosdick didn't even glance up as he penciled in a big dollar sign.

"I'm a little short of cash, John. All I got is ten dollars and change."

"That'd be a couple day's income."

"Here, dammit."

Longarm glared at the telegraph operator, but Fosdick didn't mind. He grinned as he folded the money and slipped Longarm's pocket change into his coat.

"Cigar?" Fosdick asked, needling Longarm.

"Sure, why not," Longarm growled. "Now, John, what can you tell me?"

"Only that the telegrams I sent went to Flagstaff and Prescott, Arizona."

"Do you have any names?"

"I do."

When John lit their cigars but didn't provide the names, Longarm grew irritable. "For crying out loud, who'd Cox send those telegrams to!"

"There must be a large reward for any information leading to the counterfeiter's arrest," Fosdick said, blowing a cloud of smoke over Longarm's head.

"Not that I've heard of, John. But if I hear otherwise, you'll be the first to know."

"Thanks," Fosdick said. "I might just have the key to the puzzle, and we both know that it would be worth a whole lot more than ten dollars and a handful of cheap cheroots."

"The names!"

"All right, all right." Fosdick bent over and began to rummage under the counter. "Let's see," he muttered. "I saved duplicate copies of those telegrams."

Longarm waited impatiently until Fosdick finally found the copies. Longarm eagerly read the two telegraphs over quickly, then read them again. In both cases, the telegrams were sent to land agents and stated that Cox would be arriving in Arizona and possessed funds sufficient to buy a cattle ranch. The telegrams also stated that he would be arriving to inspect ranching properties within a month.

"Well," Fosdick said, looking quite pleased with himself. "Wouldn't you say that those are pretty important leads to solving this case?"

"Can I keep them?"

"Sure. They didn't cost me anything, and I will expect you to pass my name along for at least part of that reward if Nathan Cox is apprehended in either Flagstaff or Prescott."

"I'll do what I can," Longarm said. "But I have to tell you something that you won't enjoy hearing."

Fosdick's smile wilted and he began to doodle again. "What would that be, Marshal?"

"I think these telegrams are red herrings. By that I mean that from everything I know about Nathan Cox, I'd say he is far too smart to leave any kind of paper trail that might assist a lawman to hasten his arrest."

"I disagree," Fosdick said. "At the time that he sent these, Mr. Cox was pretty loaded. He'd just lost some big bucks at the faro table and had drowned his sorrow in the best whiskey that money could buy. I can tell you this, Marshal, Cox, or whatever his name is, was in no mental shape to be acting cagey."

"I think he was probably in *excellent* mental shape and that he was pretending to be drunk in order to make us both think that he really is on his way to Arizona."

Fosdick leaned back and, for the first time ever, displayed some temper. "Now, dammit, Custis, what if you're wrong and it costs me a bundle of money!"

"Don't worry," Longarm assured the upset man. "If I am wrong and Nathan Cox really is going to Flagstaff or Prescott to buy a ranch, then you'll benefit from it. And if there is any money to be made for your information, I'll pass that right along the proper channels. You know that it doesn't matter to me one way or the other who collects the reward. It might as well be someone I like and who has been cooperative."

Fosdick relaxed. "I'm sorry I just blew up. It's just that I went and told the wife about all this, and now she's really pressuring me hard for a reward. She's even got another damned house picked out in the best part of town."

"That's unfortunate," Longarm said, "but tell her that I don't put much credence in those telegrams. From everything I've heard and seen so far about our counterfeiter, he's very smart. Sending telegrams just doesn't jibe with the kind of man who could pull off something as complex as stealing government property that could be used to create money."

"Did he get the currency plates and everything?"

"I'm afraid so," Longarm said. "Furthermore, Cox has the expertise to produce hundred-dollar bills that are identical to those in circulation."

"How many?"

"Just as many as he can spend before I catch him," Longarm answered.

"I can't imagine how the Denver mint could have been so lax in their security to allow that to happen."

"Well, John, someone has to be put in a position of trust, and Nathan Cox had earned it with years of excellent service. No one believed that he would ever risk a promising career and even go so far as to murder his federal accomplice."

"He *murdered* his accomplice?"

"That's right," Longarm said. "We don't know what happened between them. Perhaps his accomplice got cold feet and was going to turn them both in. Or maybe the accomplice even tried to murder Cox first, but whatever the reason, Cox broke the fellow's neck and took everything before he vanished in Denver.''

Fosdick shook his head. ''He was a very gracious and handsome man, Custis. I—I have to confess that he sure didn't look like a murderer.''

''What exactly,'' Longarm asked, ''is a murderer *supposed* to look like anyway?''

When John Fosdick just shook his head, Longarm continued. ''Murderers come in all shapes, ages, and sizes. I've even had to arrest some very sweet old ladies who killed their husbands or rivals. You just can't judge someone's mind or heart by their physical appearance.''

''I guess not,'' the telegraph operator said. ''Maybe I really wouldn't make a very good federal law agent. Up to now I thought that I would and, if it hadn't been for my wife, Irma, I'd have applied to become an officer.''

The man sighed. ''But now I'm just not sure if I'm not a whole lot better off being content as a simple, underpaid Western Union telegraph operator.''

''I can't answer that for you, John. But I do know this—I wouldn't be in this line of work if I had your pretty wife and a fine bunch of children.''

Fosdick managed a smile. ''Thanks. Now, I guess I better get back to work.''

Longarm nodded and went to talk to some other people whom he trusted and who might have some useful information. Because of the foul weather, it was a lousy day to be running around, but after several blind leads, Longarm found the rancher who had sold six blooded horses to Nathan Cox for a wad of worthless money. The man was hunkered up to a bar, nursing his misery.

''I was actually coming to see you federal officers,'' Dan Murphy said. ''I want some government reimbursement for my three thousand dollars worth of racing horses.''

"That's what the horses were really worth?''

"That's right,'' Murphy said, looking grim. "They were top-notch Thoroughbreds. One stallion, three mares . . . two of whom were in foal . . . and a couple of geldings.''

"They must have been pretty good horses to have had an average value of five hundred dollars each.''

"They were a bargain at that price!'' Murphy snapped as he emptied his glass. "I was strapped for cash and sold them below their true value. Any one of those horses would have brought twice that much money at a Thoroughbred auction back in Kentucky. And, as it turns out, I should have shipped them back to Kentucky and had them sold.''

"But you didn't have the money,'' Longarm said, studying the short, heavyset man in a pale brown suit and coming to the conclusion that Murphy was probably fudging the value but not his dire financial circumstances.

"That's right. So I let that fast-talking sonfabitch pass that bad money on to me.'' Murphy wiped his lips with the back of his sleeve. "Marshal, you'd better catch him, or someone like me that he's cheated will do it instead.''

"I understand,'' Longarm said. "And I also understand that you saw Cox last and that he was heading southwest.''

"That's right. He said that he wanted the horses brought out to him so that no one in Cheyenne would get any ideas about stealing, or ambushing him for them. It made sense to me, so I had them all roped together like they were on a picket line. I delivered them to Cox about three miles west of town, where the Union Pacific line spans a deep gulch. I got paid in that bad cash and he got my good horses."

"I see. Did Nathan Cox mention anything that might have given you some indication where he was heading?"

"Sure," Murphy said. "The bastard said that he was going to Arizona and that he'd probably enter a few of the horses down there in some local races. He asked me quite a few questions about which ones were the fastest, what kind of conditions they preferred to run in, and so forth. I got the impression that Cox liked to gamble and wanted to bet on his own horses for a change instead of the turn of a card or the roll of the dice."

"I see."

"So what do I do about the money I'm out?"

"Do you still have the three thousand dollars worth of counterfeit bills?"

"No, those other feds took them, but they did give me a receipt. Said that I'd be reimbursed." Murphy looked desperate. "But when?"

"I can't answer that," Longarm said honestly. "But if I were you, I'd find some way to get down to the federal mint in Denver and be first in what I expect will become a very long line of victims."

"Damn!" Murphy swore. "I know how slow the government is to release its money and how quick they are to collect. I don't need this kind of grief!"

"I'm sure you don't," Longarm said. "And I'm sorry, but the sooner that I apprehend Nathan Cox and settle this trouble, the happier we'll all be. Is there anything else that you can tell me about Cox and exactly where he might have gone?"

"Arizona. That's all."

Longarm sighed. "Maybe that's where he went ... but I doubt it. It would be too obvious."

Murphy scratched his round cheeks. "He did ask me a question that I thought was odd."

"What's that?"

"He asked me if I'd ever crossed the Wasatch Mountains."

Longarm was suddenly all ears. "The Wasatch?"

"Yeah," Murphy said. "I told him that I had and he asked me what pass I'd used."

"And you told him?"

"I told him that I'd forgotten its name but it was just west of a rough mining and logging town called Whiskey Creek over near Colorado's western border."

Murphy poured himself another drink and Longarm saw that the man's hand trembled when he said, "I remember the name of the town across the years because I drank so much whiskey myself that I staggered out of a saloon, went around behind it to throw up, and fell in that damn creek and nearly froze to death! I suspect I would have if I hadn't been so liquored up."

"Whiskey Creek. I wonder why he wanted to know about the Wasatch Mountain passes? As you well know, he wouldn't need to cross the Wasatch Mountains if he were really taking your horses down to Prescott or Flagstaff."

"You're dead right!" Murphy grunted. "If he crossed over the Wasatch into Utah, he'd sure be taking the long way around to Arizona."

"Exactly." Longarm clamped a hand on Murphy's shoulder. "You've been a lot of help."

"Where are you headed?"

"Whiskey Creek," Longarm replied. "Where else?"

"One last thing," Murphy said. "If Buck and Clyde overtake that counterfeiting sonofabitch, they won't leave enough left of him for the coyotes to chew."

"I know. I'm going to do my level best to overtake and make them understand that this is a federal matter."

"They won't listen to you," Murphy warned. "Buck and Clyde vowed to find and kill the counterfeiter. They're pretty damn good trackers as well as being first rate with a rifle or pistol."

"Thanks for the warning."

"Marshal?"

"Yeah?"

"Are you takin' that pretty woman?"

"Why do you ask?"

"Just wanted to know if she was going to decorate Cheyenne long enough for me to ask her out to dinner . . . or something."

"Sorry about that," Longarm said. "But she also lost a lot of money and won't stay behind."

"That's too bad," Murphy said. "I sure think it's a mistake to take a woman along. And if Clyde and Buck were to get the advantage on you, Marshal, there's no telling what they would do other than rape her about a hundred damned times before they killed you both."

Longarm nodded. "They'd go that far, huh?"

"Listen," Murphy said, "*they* are the ones that you ought to be worried about . . . not Cox! Clyde and Buck have bushwhacked and beaten men to death. I wouldn't want to be going after what they're after."

"I'll keep that in mind," Longarm said.

"Good luck," Murphy said as he turned and walked

away. "'Cause it sounds like you're going to need all that you can get."

"So will you with the Denver mint people," Longarm said under his breath as he went back to his hotel to get Diana Frank and start out on a muddy and miserable trail to Whiskey Creek.

Chapter 9

"They're either headin' for Whiskey Creek or else Red-cliff," Buck Zolliver shouted over the heavy downpour as he squatted in the fork of the muddy road.

"So what are we gonna do!" Clyde bellowed as thunder echoed and growled through the high Colorado mountains. "Dammit, Buck, we can't go to both places at the same time!"

Buck was the older and smarter of the brothers, but Clyde was the biggest and the meanest. "We should split up," Buck said. "Which fork do you want to ride?"

"I'll take the one leading to Whiskey Creek," Clyde decided. "It's five or six miles closer."

"Then I'll go on to Redcliff," Buck said, hauling himself into the saddle. "Whichever one of us finds that counterfeitin' bastard takes him alive and then brings him back here, where we'll meet tomorrow afternoon."

"Why here?" Clyde asked.

" 'Cause it's nowhere we can be watched," Buck told his younger brother. "And because there's some caves just up yonder that we can hole up in while we torture the bastard into tellin' us where he's stashed all that counterfeit cash."

Clyde nodded with slow understanding. Like his brother, he was a huge, lantern-jawed man with a hooked nose and heavy, brutish features. Both brothers wore full beards, dark reddish-brown, thick and coarse as the coat of a grizzly. They were sopping wet despite their oilskin slickers and their long hair hung over their collars fanning across the hump of their broad shoulders.

"If Cox is in Whiskey Creek and I get my hands on him first," Clyde promised, "I'm gonna bust up his pretty face. I'm gonna use my fists and then a knife so that no woman will ever look at him again without wantin' to empty their guts."

"Just use your hands on him, not your knife," Buck said. "If he bleeds to death, we would be out a lot of money."

"I know," Clyde said. "I just wish that fancy bastard had picked some decent weather to run off in. This storm is a real sonofabitch."

"If it snows, we've almost got him boxed in," Buck said. "The passes will close and he'll have to ride straight south. Those Thoroughbreds will slow him down. Them horses aren't up to traveling across this rough, muddy ground in foul weather."

"Let's just hope that one or the other of us finds him," Clyde said. "I'm tired of ridin' and I want to spend some of that money on those nasty Whiskey Creek women."

"If you find Cox first, tomorrow, you just bring him

back to those caves up yonder," Buck said. "Remember, we're in this together."

"Sure," Clyde said. "We're brothers."

Buck nodded and took the fork toward Redcliff. Clyde watched him disappear into the storm and then he turned his own weary horse toward Whiskey Creek. He was riding his best horse, a big roan gelding that had never quit on him no matter how hard the trail or how many the miles. But even the roan was beginning to fail. It was just plumb played out and in need of some grain and rest. Clyde liked horses and he was sorry that he'd had to push the roan so damned hard. But Whiskey Creek wasn't very far up this long mountain valley. He'd be there by midnight and he'd find the roan a livery, a stall, and some grain. And after that he'd go hunting for that shyster Nathan Cox.

"If I don't find him in town though," Clyde said to himself, "I'll find a woman and a bottle and hole up until this storm blows over."

Clyde was sure that Buck would be smart enough to do exactly the same.

The last ten miles to Whiskey Creek were a bitch, and Clyde was shaking with the cold when his exhausted roan finally staggered into town. Clyde's need for a drink and the warmth that it would bring to his innards caused him to rein up sharply before a saloon. He almost fell when he dismounted and crawled inside to stand before the bar.

"A bottle!" he roared, causing heads to turn.

"Mister," the bartender said, "you're as white as a ghost and as wet as the weather!"

"Rain is turning to sleet," Clyde said, his teeth chattering.

He drank deeply before paying for the bottle. Then he stomped back outside, and when he tried to lift his boot up to his stirrup, he was so stiff with the cold that he just couldn't cut the mustard. Taking another drink, he untied the roan from the hitching rail and led it up the sloppy street until he came to the only livery in town. The place was dark, but Clyde had dealt with old man Waite a number of times and so he unlatched the barn door and got himself and his horse in out of the freezing rain.

"Hey, Waite!" Clyde shouted, slapping at his pockets in his search for matches. "Wake up, you smelly old sonofabitch, I'm a payin' customer tonight!"

Near the back of the livery barn, a match flared and then a lantern cast its sickly grow around the inside of the huge, rickety barn. Waite emerged with a shotgun clenched in his hands. "What the hell kind of—that you, Clyde Zolliver?"

"Sure is! I need a stall for my roan horse. He's in worse shape than I am because he won't share my whiskey."

Waite lowered his shotgun. "What the hell are you doin' out in this weather so far from Cheyenne?"

"Huntin' someone."

"Couldn't it wait until the storm passed?"

"Nope." Clyde peered around the shadowy barn. "You got a lot of horses put up in here tonight."

"I'm full up."

"Then move one of 'em outside or double 'em up," Clyde ordered. "My roan is shakin' with the cold and the weariness. He needs grain and—whose tall horses *are* those?"

Waite shuffled over and raised his lantern near one of

the horses. "They're all Thoroughbreds. Fella brought 'em in two . . . no, tomorrow it'll be three days ago. Paid me a hundred gawddamn dollars! And they'll be more money comin' because—"

Clyde cut him off short. "What'd the fella look like?"

"Tall, but not quite as tall as you nor Buck. Big, but not near your size." Waite grinned. "About as handsome though."

"Did he give you his name?" Clyde asked, ignoring the man's insincere compliment.

"Nope, just his money. That's all that I needed to see. Don't need to know another damn thing about the man."

Clyde started to tell Waite that the money he'd accepted was undoubtedly counterfeit, but then he caught himself and said, "Where is this fella?"

"At the Paradise Hotel, why—is *he* the fella that you're huntin'?"

"Maybe," Clyde said evasively as he yanked his saddle and wet blanket off the roan. "Get one of them horses out of a stall so I can put my roan up before his legs drop from under him."

"Sure," Waite said, "he's shakin' pretty bad."

The transfer was made, and when the roan had been rubbed dry with gunnysacks and then fed grain and forked hay, the two men shared a few pulls on the bottle.

"I'll be back tomorrow to settle up with you," Clyde said, heading for the door.

"If you're huntin' trouble, I'd rather be paid right now," Waite complained, hurrying after the man.

"Tomorrow," Clyde growled, taking a last pull on the bottle, then handing it to the liveryman and saying, "Here, finish it off and sleep late."

"Thanks," Waite said, taking a drink. "But there

ain't a hell of a lot left and I still want to be paid.''

Clyde's expression hardened as he stood just inside the barn door glaring up the street through the falling rain. ''Old man,'' he said in a low, ominous voice, ''if you don't drop it, I'll pay you right now, all right. Only, instead of cash, I'll pay you with a gawddamn bullet!''

Waite retreated and held up one hand. ''Tomorrow will be just fine, Clyde. Just fine. I'll get that roan back in good shape. You won't even recognize him when you come back to pay me tomorrow.''

''Good,'' Clyde said, tugging the brim of his hat down over his deep-set black eyes and stomping back out into the night.

When he came to the Paradise Hotel, there was no one at the front desk, which was not the least bit surprising given the lateness of the hour. There was, however, a registration book, and Clyde turned it around and began to read the names of guests who had arrived two or three days earlier.

''Ned Cash,'' Clyde sneered, seeing that the man had been given Room 8. ''Nice touch, *Nathan Cox*.''

Clyde peeled off his rain slicker and tossed it on the floor. He removed his drooping hat and sent it spinning onto a fine leather lobby chair. Then he checked his Colt, and when he was satisfied that the gun was in good working order, headed for Room 8. Maybe he's even got a whore with him, Clyde thought happily. Maybe this is going to be a good night after all.

When he came to Nathan's room, Clyde planted his muddy boots on the carpet and pressed his ear to the door. He was disappointed not to hear the sounds of passionate lovemaking. Hell, Cox was probably just sleeping.

Clyde didn't even bother to try the knob, knowing that the counterfeiter would have the door locked. So he just reared back on one leg and kicked open the damned door. It took but an instant and then Clyde charged inside, ducking sideways out of the expected line of fire.

"Freeze or you're dead!" he shouted, cocking back the hammer of his six-gun.

They *had* been making love, by gawd! The pair of lamps on their bedside tables were flickering low but not so low that Clyde couldn't plainly see that Nathan Cox was mounted atop a big-chested woman.

The counterfeiter had turned, then froze reaching for a holstered six-gun hanging on his headboard. Clyde took three long strides and brought the barrel of his Colt slashing down across the counterfeiter's skull.

Nathan Cox groaned and collapsed on the woman, who started to scream until Clyde pointed his gun at her pretty face and said, "Open your mouth and I'll fill it with lead."

She struggled to control her terror. "Who are you?" the woman wheezed.

Clyde grabbed a handful of the counterfeiter's hair and hauled him off the woman, then rolled him to the floor. Cox still had a big, stiff rod, but it was fading fast.

Clyde chuckled, holstered his gun, and closed the door whose bolt had torn away from its latch. It was easy to fix.

"Who *are* you, mister!" the woman cried, starting to jump out of the bed and get dressed.

"Back in that bed," Clyde said, placing his hand on the butt of his gun. "Woman, you ain't goin' nowhere!"

"Please, don't hurt me!"

Clyde's eyes shifted toward the counterfeiter. "Was he good?"

The woman gulped. "I . . ."

"Was he!"

"Tears sprang to her eyes. "Yes!"

"And did he pay you with a hundred-dollar bill?"

The woman blinked with surprise. "Yes."

"Well," Clyde said, unbuckling his gun belt and letting it fall to the floor, "there's plenty more where them come from and now they all belong to *me*. You want some of what I got?"

He was already unbuttoning his muddy trousers because he knew the Whiskey Creek whore's answer would again be yes.

"Are you going to kill us?"

Clyde finished undressing. He was already stiff and long and he turned sideways so that she could really admire the enormous size of his throbbing manhood. But the woman didn't even look at the size of his cock.

"I won't say anything if you don't hurt me." Fresh tears sprang to her eyes. "Please. I don't know why you pistol-whipped him, but it has nothing to do with me."

"You're right about that," Clyde said, yanking away the sheet and blanket covering her body. "Open your legs and shut your damned mouth."

The woman did as she was told and Clyde was on her fast. He was chilled and that made her flesh seem hotter than rocks in July. Grunting and humping, he took her rough and fast, enjoying the way she whimpered even as she tried to pretend that she was enjoying the pounding.

"Who are you?" she asked when he pumped himself dry and then rolled heavily off her sweaty body.

"You don't need to know," he said. "In fact, it'd be healthier if you *didn't* know."

"Then please don't tell me."

Clyde looked around the room and spotted a bottle of high-grade brandy. "That all there is to drink in here?"

"No," she said, easing out of bed. "There's some rye whiskey in the dresser drawer."

"What else does he have in here?"

"Not much," she said. "Just a wallet full of money and his saddlebags. What were you expecting?"

"None of your damn business!"

The woman nodded. "You done with me for tonight?"

"Hell no."

"I really should go."

"Shut up."

"Are you gonna kill him?"

"No," Clyde said. "At least, not here."

"I won't say anything, mister. As far as I'm concerned, this is all just a dream."

Clyde chuckled. "A nightmare is what you really mean."

The woman did not deny the statement. "What do you want first, the rye or the brandy?"

"The brandy," he said. "Between you and the brandy, I'll finally get warmed up."

The woman nodded and went over to get the brandy. She glanced at the door and Clyde reached for his gun, saying, "You'd never make it, woman."

Sniffling, the woman returned to the rumpled bed with the bottle. "You gonna give me some of those hundred-dollar bills, mister?"

"Ha! You ain't worth a hundred dollars if I had you all month!"

She began to rub his bare chest. "You'll think a lot different come morning, mister. I promise you that."

Clyde took another drink and laughed meanly. "Then get to work," he said, grabbing her by the hair and pushing her face down between his thick legs.

The woman was good. Clyde glanced over at the unconscious Nathan Cox, and that made him feel even better. "Wish you were here too, Buck," he said. "Too damn bad that you took the road to Redcliff."

The woman looked up. "Huh?"

"It's got nothin' to do with you," Clyde told her as he spread his legs even farther apart. "I was just thinking that some people are luckier than others."

"If you pay me another hundred, we'd *both* be lucky," the woman said, looking up at him.

"Well," Clyde said, feeling like a king, "we'll just see how you do right up until morning."

Chapter 10

Rolf Swensen sat bolt upright in bed after hearing wood splintering and angry voices coming from the room next door. "Teresa, something is wrong!"

Rolf jumped out of bed naked and rushed to his door, but before he could tear it open and barge out into the hallway, Teresa grabbed his arms. "Wait!" she pleaded. "You could get yourself killed."

"Killed?" Rolf blinked in the lamplight. "Why?"

Teresa pulled him away from the door. "Because things like that happen all the time when people barge into trouble without thinking. Listen!"

They both pressed their ears to the door but heard only angry, muffled voices.

"There's definitely someone in Nathan's room that shouldn't be there," Rolf said. "He's in big trouble."

"Then so is my friend, Carole," Teresa said. "Let's just listen a moment and try to figure this out."

"*You* listen," Rolf said impatiently as he reached for the doorknob.

"Aren't you even going to arm yourself and get dressed before you go running into that room and probably get shot for your trouble?"

Rolf looked down, and his jaw dropped as he realized he was stark naked. Embarrassed, he turned away from Teresa, his cheeks coloring. "Too late, I've already seen and felt it, remember?"

"Yeah," Rolf said, blushing as he went back to the bed, sat down, and began to pull on his pants, then his shirt, and finally buckling on his six-gun.

"Well," she demanded, "do you have a plan, or are you just going to jump in there with your gun blazing?"

He looked up at her. "If you've got a better idea, Teresa, I'm all ears."

Teresa reached for her own clothes. "Carole is my best friend. If *your* friend is in trouble, then so is *my* friend, and I want to make sure we don't get them both killed. Understand?"

"Sure, but . . . but what can you do to help?"

"I'm a guaranteed male distraction. Maybe I can get in there and find out what's going on before everyone starts shooting off guns. How does that sound?"

"Sounds good," Rolf said, checking his Colt. "I don't want to kill—"

"Shhh! Listen!"

They heard more conversation. Carole sounded scared, and it seemed to Rolf that she was even pleading.

"I'm going in there now," Rolf said, yanking on his boots, "before your friend and my friend are *dead* friends."

"No!"

Teresa lowered her voice. "Just let me finish pulling on my dress and stockings and patching myself up a little, and I'll find out what is wrong. If I can, I'll talk the man outside and you can get the drop on him in the hallway."

"And if you can't?" Rolf asked.

Teresa thought about that a moment, then said, "I'll kick the wall or the door or something. That will be the signal for you to come in with your six-gun ready."

"You're taking a big, big risk."

"Carole is worth it," Teresa said, "and you must think that your friend is too, or we'd still be humping in bed."

"Yeah," he said, "I guess that's true enough. But I think you are awfully brave."

"Brave?" Teresa smiled. "In my business, you had better be a little brave or you'll soon be dead."

Rolf watched her finish dressing. He had an over-powering desire to tell Teresa that he'd fallen in love with her and wanted her to be his bride. But Rolf was so nervous that he couldn't get all that out just then so instead, he just grabbed and kissed Teresa.

"Hey!" she cried, pushing him back and staring at him as if he'd gone crazy. "What's the matter with you anyway? This is no time for that!"

"I know," he said, feeling real stupid. "But I couldn't help myself. I'm in love with you and . . . if I was to get killed in a few minutes, I wanted you to know my heart."

Her anger melted and Teresa's face softened. She came over, put her arms around his neck, and said, "Rolf, you really mean that, don't you?"

"Darn right! I love you, Teresa, but I'm no kid."

"I believe it. And I almost believe that I could love you too."

Rolf almost dropped his gun. "Then you'll marry me!"

Teresa didn't know whether to weep or to laugh. She did neither. "Rolf, honey," she said, "this has been one of the strangest nights of my whole sorry life. And I don't know *what* kind of trouble is going on next door or what will happen to us now. But trust me, I'm far more experienced in these matters than you are, and I should try to get into that room and find out what we're up against."

He kissed her again. "But what if you get shot?"

"Then I would either die or survive."

"But—"

"Shhh! Don't ask any more questions. Just be ready in case I can't handle the trouble."

"All right," he heard himself tell her. "I'll be ready and I won't miss if it comes to shooting. I'm a dead shot, Teresa. I may look harmless, but I'm not."

"Okay," she whispered, breaking free of his arms. "Let's get this over with."

Rolf gripped his six-gun so tightly that his hand ached and his fingers started to go numb. Aware that his hand might actually lock up, he tried to relax as Teresa stepped out into the hallway and then knocked on the broken but closed door to Nathan's room.

"Who is it!" Clyde roared.

"It's Teresa!"

"Go away! I already got a whore!"

"I need to speak to Carole!"

"We're busy!"

Teresa took a deep breath and banged harder on the

door. "Carole! Carole, are you all right!"

"I said to go away!"

"I *have* to see my friend!"

Rolf heard Carole cry out in pain, and then he actually felt the floor shake under the feet of whoever it was that had barged into Nathan's room. Rolf stepped back into his own room, gun up and ready to fire as Nathan's broken door was yanked open. Out in the hallway, Teresa also took an involuntary step backward and her hand flew to her lips. Rolf could see Teresa, but not the man she faced, although he must have been pretty threatening, because Teresa suddenly looked very frightened.

"Clyde?" she whispered.

Rolf knew at once that she was facing Clyde Zolliver and had every reason to be terrified.

Clyde's laugh filled the dim hallway. "Yeah, Teresa, baby. I knew you'd never forget old Clyde and that long night we had together."

Teresa visibly shivered and then attempted to look past the giant whose form was blocking the doorway. "Please, can I see Carole now?"

"Why, sure! If I knowed it was my little spitfire out here, I'd have come running. Join our party! I got plenty of meat for the both of you whores."

"That's not what I want."

"Don't matter what you want," he said threateningly. "It never has and it never will. There's only one thing that you'll ever be any good for, so come on in and let's do it."

Rolf watched as the woman he loved began to retreat across the hallway. She looked petrified as she made one last attempt to lean around Clyde's big body and call, "Carole, are you all right!"

"Yes, but run!"

Teresa's back met the far hallway as Clyde towered over her. He was huge and muscular and his manhood was up and poking Teresa. Rolf knew Clyde and his brother. He'd seen the both of them several times, and he'd heard stories of how brutal and dangerous they were.

"Please," Teresa said, "just let Carole go."

"She don't *want* to go," Clyde said, chuckling obscenely. "I'm payin' her well, but she's getting tired. I think you should spell your little friend for the rest of the night."

Teresa looked up, her eyes filled with hatred. "Don't even touch me, you horrible sonofabitch! I told you what I'd do if you ever touched me again."

Clyde reached down and grabbed his big root. "Yeah, and that's why I'm going to give this tonight. And I'll do it right here against this wall if you don't shut up and come inside."

Rolf took a deep breath and filled his own doorway. "Clyde Zolliver, you aren't doing anything to anyone anymore," he said in a voice shrill with fear.

Clyde swung around, his hand still wrapped around his root. He stared and said, "Say, ain't you that kid named . . ."

"Swensen. Rolf Swensen. It's only fair that you know who killed you."

Clyde started to let go of himself and lunge, but Rolf had anticipated the man's reaction, and his finger was already squeezing his trigger. An explosion filled the hallway, and Rolf's bullet went low, catching Clyde in the groin. The big man howled and tried to lunge forward, but Rolf raised the barrel of his pistol and shot him in the chest, knocking him back a step and jerking him up to attention.

"Gawddamn you, kid!" Clyde choked.

Rolf stood his ground and emptied his gun, placing his bullets in the giant's hairy chest and driving him back through his own broken doorway. When Clyde toppled, he landed like a big tree, and then his bare heels danced spasmodically on the floor. Clyde's stiff root momentarily waved around like a flag in battle before it slumped over as dead as the man.

"Holy gawd," Rolf said, slumping against the doorway as Teresa threw herself into his arms. "I really did it. I *killed* Clyde Zolliver and now his brother and father will kill me."

"No, they won't!" Teresa said fiercely as she was joined by Carole. "We're going away."

"I'm going too!" Carole said, twisting around to stare at the dead man. "I'm not staying in Whiskey Creek another day!"

"What about Nathan?" Rolf asked, steadying himself and holding his girl tightly. "Is he . . . dead?"

"No, but he's knocked out cold. Clyde pistol-whipped him hard. I don't know, maybe he'll die or his brains have been scrambled. I just don't know!"

"I'll find a doctor," Rolf heard himself say as people began to open their doors and peek down the hallway.

"It's over!" Teresa raged at them. "So just go back to sleep!"

One by one the doors closed. Teresa hurried inside, and all three of them hovered anxiously over Nathan as Teresa examined the unconscious counterfeiter.

"Well?" Rolf asked.

"He's breathing and his pulse is good," Teresa said.

117

"I think he's going to be all right."

"Maybe not," Carole said. "You didn't see how that big sonofabitchin' Clyde just mashed his skull. He hit him really hard."

"We had better not move him yet," Teresa said. "But there's no real doctor in Whiskey Creek."

"No doctor?" Rolf began to reload his gun. "Nathan could die without a doctor."

But Teresa shook her head. "I don't think there's anything even a real doctor could do."

"So what can we do besides just wait?" Rolf asked as he finished reloading and jamming his six-gun back into his holster.

Carole interrupted. "The first thing we ought to do is to find somewhere to hide Clyde's body. Somewhere that it won't ever be found."

"You're right," Teresa said, thinking hard. "I know of an abandoned mine. It's a vertical shaft that drops about a hundred feet straight down. People sometimes throw dead things in it just to get rid of them."

"But we should at least bury him," Rolf said, appalled at the idea of pitching a human body into a disposal pit filled with all manner of ungodly things.

"Rolf, if it would make you feel any better," Teresa said, "we can throw some rocks in after we dump his body. But I'll have to find us a wagon or a carriage."

"What about the hotel clerk and—"

"Peter acts uppity," Carole said, "and he must have heard all the shouting and your gunshots, but you don't see a trace of him, do you?"

"No."

"That's because he's a rabbit," Carole said, making no effort to conceal her disgust. "Peter won't come up here and he won't ask any questions. Not about the blood on the hotel carpets and not about the broken latch on Nathan's door."

"Good," Rolf said.

"Let's go," Teresa said. "I'll help you drag his body down the back stairs leading into the alley."

"I think we ought to at least put some pants on him," Rolf said, staring uneasily at the bloody giant's naked body.

"No!" Carole's eyes blazed away at the corpse. "Rolf," she said, "you just toss Clyde down in the pit naked. If there are snakes, bugs, worms, or rats, all I want them to do is chew his damn cock off!"

Rolf shuddered and turned away from Carole. He could only imagine how much hatred both women had for Clyde Zolliver.

It took Rolf and Teresa an hour to borrow a buckboard and drive through the stormy night. Twice, they almost got stuck in the mud, but they finally managed to reach the pit and dump Clyde's body into it. Rolf and Teresa both heard the corpse ricochet off the walls all the way down, and then they heard a tremendous splash as it struck bottom.

Rolf shivered. "With all this rain, the bottom of the pit must be filled with water."

"Good! Clyde!" she yelled down into the black hole. "I hope you have to swim your way into hell!"

Rolf pulled Teresa away and then led her back to the buckboard. With the thunder and lightning all around, they drove away quickly. They did not speak at first, just sat close, their heads huddled low in the pouring rain. Rolf had never seen such hatred in his life. Rolf was badly shaken. He hadn't believed that a woman could feel such deep hatred, a hatred every bit as alive and intense as any man's.

"Rolf?" she asked as they neared Whiskey Creek and the rain let up a little.

"Yeah?"

"Did you mean it earlier tonight when you said you were going to California and wanted to marry me?"

"I did."

"Do you still? I mean, after seeing the . . . the really terrible side of me?"

Rolf thought a moment or two before answering, then he looked sideways at Teresa and said, "We all have a dark side. Maybe it was good that I saw yours right away. Maybe you think I'm better than I am too."

She hugged him tightly. "Rolf, there's a side that I didn't think you possessed."

"Which side is that?"

"It was a *strong* side. A side that allowed you to just stand there and keep pumping bullets into Clyde, knowing how evil he was. It made me look at you differently, Rolf. It opened my eyes."

"Does that mean we're getting married?" he asked as the buckboard slid around a muddy street corner and Rolf turned it back into the alley behind their hotel.

She kissed his cheek. "It does, if Buck or his father don't catch and kill us."

Rolf smiled, and his eyes burned with tears so that he was thankful for the rain. With a close friend in Nathan Cox and a woman he loved with all his heart and had just consented to become his wife, everything in his life was now much, much different. And if he really was forced to do it, Rolf vowed he would somehow find a way to kill Buck and even old man Zolliver.

120

Chapter 11

Longarm was damned glad that the rain finally stopped falling and the skies had turned blue. It was cold though. He and Miss Diana Frank were bundled up in heavy coats and rain slickers, but they were still plenty chilly. There was snow atop the higher elevations of the Wasatch Mountains, and Longarm couldn't help but think that Nathan Cox might have gotten trapped up there in this last storm and frozen to death along with the Thoroughbreds. That being the case, Longarm might not be able to recover their bodies or the stolen Denver mint plates and counterfeit currency until the next spring.

"How much farther to Whiskey Creek?" Diana asked, her face pale and windburned.

"Must be just up ahead," Longarm said. "Yonder comes a rider. Maybe he'll know."

The rider was a cowboy nursing a broken arm, a broken nose, and cracked ribs. His face was swollen and purplish, his eyes filled with pain, and he was headed for Cheyenne.

"My name is Arnie and I worked for a spread called the Swinging T Ranch for three years," the suffering cowboy explained without preamble. "I was their top hand! Only one who could bust the bad outlaw broncs that the owner kept trying to turn into cow ponies."

"Is that what happened to you?" Diana asked. "You got stomped or thrown by a bronc?"

"Naw! I got into a fistfight about a week ago with a man named Buck Zolliver over in Redcliff. He was drunk and raisin' hell with everyone. He slapped a saloon gal named Janice so hard, it broke her lips like they was stomped grapes. I went crazy and attacked the big bastard."

"Sounds like you made a bad mistake," Longarm said, wanting to hear all that he could about Buck Zolliver.

"Yeah, it was a big mistake all right. Buck beat the livin' shit outa me. He broke my nose with an overhand right that drove me through the back wall of the saloon. When I tried to get up and run, he landed on me with both knees and cracked every rib. He kept hitting me in the face so that most of my teeth are either gone or loose."

"He sounds like a bad one," Longarm said grimly.

"He is! I had some friends with enough guts to pull him off of me, but they say he stomped my leg as he was being hauled off my poor, quiverin' body. They say he was screamin' like a man gone crazy. I know he'd have killed me in a few more minutes. I never been hit so damned hard in my life!"

"Is he still in the town of Redcliff?"

"Hell," the cowboy said between still puffy lips, "I don't know! Janice took me in and nursed me awhile. She's a whore, but she has a good heart and I always liked her a lot. I guess I stayed with her about a week before she gave me some money and told me to ride out and find some other friends."

"And that's why you're headed for Cheyenne?" Diana asked.

"Yep. I got some people that will winter me up and I hope to be fit enough to cowboy next spring. I don't know though. I suspect I'll never be patched up enough to bust broncs again. Everyone says I'm lucky just to be alive."

"Maybe you are," Longarm said, thinking that it had been a long time since he'd seen anyone so badly beaten.

"But I'd like to kill Buck," Arnie growled. "Why, wouldn't you if some giant sonofabitch beat you and then tried to kill you with his bare hands?"

"Yeah," Longarm admitted, "I suppose I would."

"I been whipped bad and I've won my share of fights," Arnie said with a sad shake of his head. "But I *never* been beaten like that. When I woke up in Janice's little room, first thing I tried to do was climb to my feet, get a gun, and go huntin' for Buck Zolliver. I'd kill him in a minute if I got him in my sights."

"Why *didn't* you go looking for him?" Longarm asked.

"He'd left town early the next morning. Everyone said he rode over to Whiskey Creek. I heard that he was looking for his kid brother, Clyde. Clyde is said to be even meaner and tougher than Buck, but I don't believe that. Buck could whip any man alive, but someone will put a bullet in him one of these days. You don't fight a man like Buck Zolliver with your hands. You go at him with a gun, or a singletree or, if you feel brave, a damn big club!''

Arnie swallowed. ''I want to find Buck and settle the score, but I'm not much good with a gun and I heard that he's real good. So Janice made me promise just to go to Cheyenne. But she didn't know that's where Buck and his accursed family is from. I expect that I'll meet up with Buck this winter or next spring and that I'll shoot him on sight.''

''That could get you hanged,'' Longarm said.

''Maybe,'' Arnie said, ''but after someone does what Buck Zolliver did to Janice and me . . . well, it'd be about worth it.''

Longarm leaned on his saddle horn. ''Did you ever hear of a man named Nathan Cox?''

''No,'' Arnie said. ''What's he look like?''

Longarm provided a description, but Arnie just shook his head. ''I'd have remembered him and those Thoroughbred horses. I'm awful mindful of horses. I forget faces, but not horses, and I'd have remembered if he'd come to Redcliff.''

''Thanks,'' Longarm said, lifting his reins. ''I sure hope that you get mended.''

''Oh, I will,'' Arnie promised. ''You going to Redcliff, or to Whiskey Creek?''

''Whiskey Creek.''

''It can't be more than two, maybe three hours up ahead. Just keep to the right when the road forks.''

''Thanks.''

Arnie started to lift his reins, but then he said, ''Mister, you and the lady might even hear a song about me someday if I get hanged for gunning Buck Zolliver down.''

"I hope not,'' Longarm said.

Arnie wiped a battered hand across his eyes. He looked ready to topple off his horse into the mud. "Mister,'' he asked, "why are you so curious about Buck and this Nathan Cox?''

"I got my reasons,'' Longarm said, touching his heels to the flanks of his horse. "So long, Arnie. Just forget about Buck Zolliver and find a good cowboying job next spring.''

"Well,'' Arnie said, looking sick and depressed, "I can't rest until I settled my score.''

"Maybe,'' Longarm said as he rode away, "I'll have to do it for you.''

"You mean that!'' Arnie managed a lopsided grin.

"Maybe,'' Longarm called back as he and Diana put their horses into a ground-eating trot down the muddy road toward Whiskey Creek.

When they reached that mountain settlement, Longarm rode down the center of the street and made sure that there wasn't a marshal's office to visit first.

"This town looks rough as a cob,'' Longarm said as hard faces stared out through saloon and poor-looking little business doorways.

"Nice enough looking hotel though,'' Diana said, pointing toward the Paradise. "Can we stay there, Custis? I really need a bath and a soft, dry bed.''

Longarm needed them too, but he said, "Diana, you told me just a couple of nights ago that you were satisfied in any bed that we shared.''

She stared at him. "*I* actually said something that stupid?''

125

"You did."

"I must have been half asleep."

"Nope, wide awake," he told her. "And purrin' beside me like a milk-fed kitten."

"Well," Diana said, knowing that he was teasing her. "I have said a lot of foolish things in my lifetime. And while I love you in bed, what I really need is sleep."

"We'll stay the night at the Paradise Hotel," Longarm said. "I'm going to have to use a counterfeit hundred and get some change for travelin', but the federal government can reimburse the hotel later."

"Thanks," Diana breathed with obvious relief.

Longarm normally took care of his horses first, but Diana looked so exhausted by the cold and the long trail that he took mercy on her and went to check into the hotel. The clerk gave them a room and didn't say a word about the crisp counterfeit hundred-dollar bill, although Longarm saw that he gave it a pretty thorough inspection.

After taking Diana up to their room and seeing that a hot bath was on its way for them both, Longarm went back outside and took their horses to the town's only real livery.

"Two dollars a day per horse," the grumpy-looking old man said. "Paid in advance."

"Sure thing," Longarm said, paying the man and then adding another dollar, hoping to grease the old liveryman's tongue. The extra dollar worked, as it generally did.

"Stranger, where you from?" the liveryman asked.

"Cheyenne," Longarm said. "I'm looking for a friend of mine. A fella named Nathan Cox."

The liveryman shook his head. "Must be a stranger

too, 'cause I never even heard of him, and I know everyone in Whiskey Creek."

Longarm described Cox and, as he did so, could see a change come over the liveryman.

"Sorry," the liveryman said, abruptly turning to leave, "but I got work to do."

"But have you seen the man I described? He had at least six blooded Thoroughbreds and I'm sure he would have had to bring them here if he was passing through."

"Well, then I guess he wasn't passing through!" the liveryman said, unwilling to meet Longarm eye to eye.

"I think he was," Longarm said, having no choice but to drag out his badge. "And as a lawman, I'm strongly suggesting that you be honest and tell me what happened here. Otherwise I might have to take you back to Denver."

"On what charge?"

"Withholding important information relating to an outlaw wanted by the federal government."

"All right," the liveryman, Waite, finally said, looking whipped. "But, Marshal, I had no part in any of this and I want that understood from the start."

"Fair enough. I just want to find Nathan Cox."

"He's gone," the liveryman flatly stated. "He came in here with another young fella named Rolf Swensen. Swensen is just a would-be cowboy. A nobody. They were travelin' together and the pair seemed friendly enough toward each other, though you'd be hard pressed to find bigger opposites."

"Go on."

"Well, Clyde Zolliver came in a couple days after they hit town and hooked up with a pair of whores."

"Clyde, or Nathan Cox and this Swensen fellow?"

"Nathan and Rolf Swensen," the old man said. "The dandy seemed to have all the money in the world. He wanted the best that Whiskey Creek could offer, which ain't much. But the whores whose names were Teresa and Carole, they were pretty slick for a place like this and there were a lot of cowboys that got upset when all their time was bought up by that pair."

"Then what happened?"

"Clyde Zolliver arrived and went after 'em. The next thing I know, everyone was gone."

Longarm thumbed back the brim of his hat. "What do you mean, gone?"

"Just what I said, Marshal! There was a big gunfight over at the Paradise Hotel. People ain't saying much about it, but I gather that the kid gunned Clyde down in the hall. They say he was naked as a snake when he got drilled about five times. I guess it was a hell of a bloody battle."

Longarm hadn't expected to hear anything like this. "So the kid killed Clyde Zolliver?" he asked.

"That's right! The witnesses say that they were ordered back into their rooms in no uncertain terms. When they came out the next morning, Cox, the kid, and the two whores were all gone. Their horses were gone from this barn too."

"They just . . . just vanished?"

"Sure. Why not? There's no law in Whiskey Creek, and the weather was so bad that nobody even thought to go after them. I was well paid and they left a hundred dollars extra for a buckboard and a set of old harness. Must have harnessed one of their saddle horses and all skedaddled in the storm just before sunrise."

"Well, I'll be damned!" Longarm said.

"You may be damned," Waite said, breaking into a self-satisfied grin, "but I'm happy. You see, I made two hundred dollars! 'Course, some of it was for hay and grain. I fed them Thoroughbreds more than any animals had a right to eat while they were here. But the buckboard wasn't worth but about fifty dollars and the harness another ten. So I made forty dollars clear profit on that deal and some extra on the horses. I hope Cox and the kid ride through again and we do the same thing all over."

Longarm didn't have the heart to tell the old man that his two hundred dollars were probably counterfeit. The hell with that. Longarm knew that he had enough trouble without upsetting everyone who had been slicked by the Denver counterfeiter.

"Where would you guess that they were heading?"

The liveryman spat a stream of tobacco juice at the dirt. "You know something, Marshal, Buck Zolliver seemed almighty interested in my answer to that very same question."

"He's still here?"

"That's right. But I'd sure give Buck a wide berth. You see, he's lookin' for his brother's body. Been lookin' for a couple of days now. He's drunk and crazy with anger. This is a real rough town, and there are some bad men in Whiskey Creek, but they're staying out of Buck Zolliver's way. I'd advise you to do the very same."

"Thanks for the advice," Longarm said. "It doesn't make any sense that they'd take Clyde's body too far."

"I can't figure that either," Waite said. "Even in this cold weather, it'd get to smellin' real rank in a couple of days."

"So where would you go to dispose of a body?"

"Like I told Buck, I'd dump it down a mine shaft so that no one would ever find it. Marshal, there are at least ten deep shafts within two miles of Whiskey Creek. My guess is that Clyde's body is floating at the bottom of one of them and that it will never be found."

Longarm shook his head. "Looks like both Buck and I have come to a dead end."

"I kind of liked that Cox fella. I don't understand why he let the kid do his killing up in that hotel, but you might want to give that one some thought. Also, women don't travel this hard country too fast, and they'll be riding in my old buckboard."

"Good points to remember," Longarm said.

"You gonna pay me another dollar for the extra information?" Waite asked, spitting tobacco between their feet.

"Nope," Longarm said, "because it sounds like you are one hell of a lot richer than most of us poor working folks."

"Yep," Waite said, hooking his thumbs into the top of his dirty bib coveralls, "I expect that I am."

Before Longarm stepped outside, he turned back to the liveryman and said, "I ain't going to pay you extra, but do you know where I can find Buck Zolliver?"

"Any saloon where other people ain't," Waite told him. "Buck is in a killin' frame of mind, and people are scattering when he comes around. You just peek inside a few saloons, and when you see an empty one, that'll be where you'll find Buck."

"Thanks," Longarm said.

"You gonna try and kill Buck?"

"Nope," Longarm said as he headed into the muddy

street, "not unless he tries to kill me first."

"He will!" Waite called. "The Zollivers *hate* lawmen!"

"I'll keep that in mind!" Longarm called back as marched back toward the hotel with his hand not far from his gun.

Chapter 12

"I'm scared," Diana said, watching as Longarm checked his gun. "What if you get killed?"

"Then make sure that the federal government gives me a decent burial," Longarm said, trying hard to sound lighthearted. "But don't let them bury me in this hellhole of a town."

"I'm serious!" Diana wailed.

"So am I."

Satisfied that his gun was ready and that the derringer he kept attached to his watch chain was also in good working order, Longarm went to the woman and tried to calm her fears.

"There's no real danger in this," he began, "because—"

"No danger! Custis, you said that entire saloons full of hard men emptied at the mere sight of Buck Zolliver."

"All right, so he's on the prod," Longarm conceded, "but I have all the advantages because he doesn't know that I'm a lawman. And besides, all that I really want to do is question the man. I mean, to my knowledge, he hasn't done anything wrong."

"His brother was gunned down! He's after the same man we're after."

"That's not against the law," Longarm said.

Diana heaved a deep sigh. "Can't we just leave in the morning without you questioning this brute?"

"No," Longarm said. "Because if we did that, then he'd be on our backtrail and I'd always be looking over my shoulder. I need to know where he stands before we leave Whiskey Creek."

"He stands to kill Nathan and his new friend! And anyone else that comes between him and vengeance. Custis, surely you can see that."

Longarm gave her a comforting hug. "Listen, Diana," he said, "I'm not worried about Buck Zolliver and you shouldn't be either. I am, however, worried about overtaking Nathan Cox and putting his money-making machine out of business before he bankrupts the federal government."

"He's not doing *that* much counterfeiting."

"Not yet," Longarm agreed, "but that's only because he hasn't settled down so that he can really get his operation in gear. Up to now, Nathan Cox has been on the move. That will change when he buys his ranch or whatever it is he intends to buy in order to settle down and get serious about counterfeiting."

"I don't see how you can be so sure of that."

"I've been chasing outlaws and con artists long enough to be able to read their minds. If I couldn't do

133

that, I wouldn't be much good in this business."

Diana sighed. "All right. Go and see this monster and have your talk. But if you get yourself killed, it's your own damn fault."

"Right," Longarm said, reaching for his hat and then heading for the door.

It took Longarm just fifteen minutes to locate Buck, who had taken over the run-down and all but vacant Antelope Saloon. The only one in the place besides Buck was the owner, who doubled as the bartender. He was a frightened-looking man with a handlebar mustache and a dirty white shirt. When Longarm stepped into the silent establishment, the poor man actually tried to wave him back outside.

"Howdy," Longarm said, his eyes flicking toward the bartender but then coming to rest on Buck. "You *are* open for business, aren't you?"

The owner nodded. "Yeah," he said, "but you might find it a little healthier to move on, mister."

Buck was giving Longarm the evil eye. His face was bloated from heavy drinking and he looked huge, menacing, and dissipated. Longarm had expected a big man, but not *this* big.

"Howdy!" Longarm called over at Buck. "You interested in a game of poker?"

"Leave me the hell alone!" Buck roared.

The saloon owner's hand trembled when he laid it down on the bar top. "Mister," he said under his breath, "I really appreciate you comin' into my place, but I think—"

"It's going to be all right," Longarm assured the man behind the bar. "I just come in for a shot of whiskey and some friendly conversation. Last time I was in here, the place was real busy. What happened to everyone?''

''They were afraid of catching *lead* poisoning,'' Buck growled. ''And you might want to get your ass outa here before you catch a case of it yourself.''

''Aw,'' Longarm said, motioning for the bartender to leave a bottle and a glass. Pouring himself a shot, Longarm continued with a shrug and a smile, ''I'm not too worried. You see, I'm not looking for trouble. I just want something to drink, a little friendly conversation, and a card game.''

''Get outa here!''

Longarm tossed down his drink and refilled his glass. Carrying both the bottle and the shot glass across the room, he came to a halt in front of Buck's table. ''You look like you're out of sorts, mister. Can I buy you a drink?''

Buck lurched to his feet, and Longarm judged him to be at least six foot six inches and nearly three hundred pounds—all of it mean.

''I'm going to give you to the count of three to get your stupid ass outa this saloon!'' Buck warned. ''And after that, you're going to be fitted for a pine box.''

''Is that right?''

''Yeah! One. Two—''

Longarm tossed his glass of whiskey into Buck's sodden face. When the man clawed for his gun, Longarm swung the whiskey bottle and struck him right between the eyes. The bottle shattered and both whiskey and blood flowed. Buck staggered, then lunged forward with a roar and would have gotten ahold of Longarm if the table hadn't gotten in his way and tripped him to the dirty sawdust floor.

Longarm kicked the man hard, his boot snapping

Buck's head back hard enough to break a man's neck.

"Why don't we just have us a nice little talk?" Longarm said as Buck struggled to stand.

Buck came off the floor with both hands filled with sawdust, which he hurled into Longarm's face. When Longarm tried to clear his vision, Buck hit him with a thundering overhand that drove Longarm over another card table and sent him skidding across the sawdust.

"Damn," Longarm swore groggily as Buck swung a boot at his face. Longarm rolled sideways and felt the wind move beside his cheek. He could have drawn his gun, but Longarm had a strong urge to see if he could whip this big bastard with his fists.

"You had your chance," Buck snarled, throwing himself at Longarm before he could stand.

Most men would have fallen away from the giant's charge, but Longarm did the opposite and tackled Buck. The giant landed hard, breath gushing from his lungs. An instant later Longarm pounded the man in the side of the face and knocked him flat. Buck lay still for a moment, then spat out a bloody molar and swayed erect.

"I'm going to kill you with my bare hands," Buck vowed, raising his fists and squinting through an eye that was already beginning to swell shut.

"Maybe you ought to just have another drink and rethink that decision," Longarm said, raising his own fists.

Buck lunged, clumsily feinting a left cross. Buck attempted to follow with a looping right that Longarm avoided while he landed two thundering uppercuts to the giant's gut. Buck's mouth flew open, and he gasped for air even as Longarm stepped back and broke the big man's hanging jaw.

Buck roared and his knees buckled. Longarm waded

in with both fists flying and drove the bigger man backward in choppy steps until Buck was pinned against the bar.

"Stop!" Buck wailed. "I'm whipped!"

"Not yet, you aren't," Longarm said between clenched teeth as he sledged a punch to Buck's ribs that doubled the giant up in pain. Then, grabbing Buck's right arm and raising it overhead, Longarm slammed the big man's right arm down on the edge of the bar, hearing the forearm bones crack like a thick limb.

Buck screamed and collapsed. "No more! Please!"

"Is that what the cowboy named Arnie said as you tried to beat him to death!" Longarm shouted. "Is it!"

Buck bowed his head and whimpered.

Longarm stepped back, wiping his bloody knuckles on his shirt, then glancing over at the bartender. "A bottle and two glasses," he ordered.

"Yes, sir!" the man shouted, trying to hide his joy at this unexpected turn of events.

Longarm didn't have to pour the drinks, because the bartender did that for him. Crouching beside the suffering man, Longarm handed him a glass and said, "Drink up, Buck, it will ease your pain."

"Who *are* you, gawddamit!"

"United States Marshal Custis Long. And I'm here to give you fair warning that you had better give up the chase for Nathan Cox and return to Cheyenne."

"I'm going to *kill* Cox and that Swensen kid!" Buck choked.

"No, you're not," Longarm said. "And if you don't give up this chase, I might have to kill you."

"They murdered my brother!"

"Maybe," Longarm said, "but from everything I've

137

heard so far, it sounds like Clyde got exactly what he deserved.''

Buck pulled himself up using the edge of the bar. He swayed and glared hatefully at Longarm. ''So,'' he said, ''you're a gawddamn United States marshal, huh?''

''That's right.''

''Good,'' Buck said, turning away and staggering toward the front door, ''that'll make it all even sweeter.''

Longarm was a decisive man, and he was pretty sure from Buck's comment that the giant had no intention of giving up the deadly game. But without proof, there was nothing he could do, because this was a free country.

Longarm strode outside and yelled at Buck Zolliver. ''If you come after me, I'll use my gun instead of my fists! You hear me!''

Zolliver turned and Longarm's hand automatically dropped to the butt of his six-gun. But the giant couldn't make a play because of his now-broken right arm. Instead, he just spat blood and shook like he had the ague, only it was hatred and not a fever that was causing his huge body to quiver.

After a moment Buck turned and continued on. Longarm watched the giant disappear around a corner.

''Well,'' Longarm muttered sarcastically to himself, ''I sure took care of that matter like a veteran lawman.''

''Marshal?''

Longarm turned around to see the saloon owner. ''Yeah?''

''My name is Terrence and I got some prime whiskey that I save just for special occasions. What you did just now was a *very* special occasion. Would you join me in a couple of drinks? I'd consider it an honor to drink to the man that whipped Buck Zolliver and drove him the hell outa my saloon."

"Yeah," Longarm said, rubbing his own aching jaw. "I'll join you in a drink."

Longarm was soon feeling a lot better. Not only was the whiskey as excellent as promised, but he was learning a little more about the kid named Rolf Swensen and the two women who'd also left town with Nathan Cox.

"Carole and Teresa were whores, but they were a real cut above the average," Terrence said. "I tried like hell to get them to come to work for me behind this bar, but they wouldn't. They chose to work in a bigger place that could pay them more. I understood, but I sure would have liked to have them working for me."

"Did Clyde come in here before he was shot to death in the hallway?"

"Nope," Terrence said, "he went straight to the Paradise Hotel, near as I can figure. He was a real bad one. Even worse than Buck."

"I met their father in Cheyenne," Longarm said. "And having met Emmett Zolliver, I can understand why those two boys were so mean."

"Buck ain't done with you or those others," Terrence warned. "I can tell you that for a fact."

"Well," Longarm said, "I told him that I'd shoot him if he tried to follow us. I'll not have a bushwhacker like that on my backtrail."

"You should have broke his neck when you had the chance," Terrence said, clucking his tongue. "Buck Zolliver is the kind of enemy that you have in your worst nightmare. I was the only witness and I damn sure would have said that you killed Buck in self-defense."

Longarm emptied his fourth glass of whiskey.

"Well," he said, "I am sworn to uphold the law. That means bringing the guilty in for trial, not executing them, no matter how much they might deserve that fate."

Terrence nodded. He was drinking pretty fast, and Longarm could well imagine that the saloon owner was letting off a lot of pent-up rage and tension. It could not have been nice with Buck as his only customer.

"Marshal?"

"Yeah?"

"As long as I live, I'll never see a more vicious fistfight than the one that you and Buck had a little while ago. And I'd not have believed that anyone could whip him . . . except maybe his own brother."

"Buck was half drunk," Longarm said, voicing his own thoughts on the matter. "If he'd have been completely sober, it would have been a lot rougher. Buck's reactions were shot and his punches slow and wide. If he'd have been sober, I think I'd have had no choice but to go for my gun instead of giving him a whipping."

"Like he gave to that cowboy named Arnie."

"Yeah," Longarm said, deciding that he had better return to the hotel and a very worried Diana Frank. "So long, Terrence. Thanks for the fine whiskey."

"Anytime you're passing through, the drinks are free in your case," Terrence said. "And I'm not just saying that because I'm on my way to getting looped either. I mean it! As long as I own this place, if you come here, you drink free."

Longarm smiled, but then winced with pain. "That guy sure had a punch," he said.

"Watch out for him, Marshal. Buck will be coming

after you as soon as he sobers up and can stand to ride a horse.''

Longarm supposed that was true as he walked back to the hotel and rejoined Diana, who had been soaking in a hot tub of bathwater but was now standing naked and dripping before him.

''Darling! I thought you might be dead by now! Oh,'' she cried, ''look what happened to your poor, battered face!''

''It's all right,'' Longarm said, glancing over the tub. ''I'm just a little sore and a little drunk. Help me get undressed and into that tub to soak.''

Diana helped him and then, when his chin began to dip and he started to fall asleep in the bath, she pulled him out, dried him off, and put him to bed, where he slept like the dead until ten o'clock the following morning.

Chapter 13

Since leaving Whiskey Creek on the run almost two weeks earlier, Rolf Swensen wasn't exactly sure what was going to happen from one day to the next. Nathan hadn't recovered from his pistol-whipping, and although it was clear that he would survive, Rolf's new friend remained dazed and disoriented. It was a frightening thing to see Nathan suffer so, and Rolf didn't know what to do to help him. Carole and Teresa helped take care of Nathan, but neither of them knew where they were going or for what purpose save covering enough ground so that a Zolliver didn't overtake and kill them all.

"Poor Nathan needs to see a good brain specialist," Carole kept repeating. "A real doctor who can tell us what has happened to his mind."

"It got scrambled," Teresa said. "You said that Clyde pistol-whipped him real hard. Clyde was awful

142

strong. I think Nathan's mind was scrambled like an egg.''

"Don't say that!'' Carole protested. "Nathan will be all right. He just needs some time. He's getting better and better every day.''

"No, he's not,'' Teresa argued. "His color is good, but he doesn't say anything. I'm not even sure that he *thinks* anything.''

"Of course he does!'' Carole cried. "He's just . . . just confused.''

And so the pair would argue, leaving poor Rolf to wonder who was right and what was going to become of them. He had found the United States mint's property in Nathan's packs and was shocked to realize that his best friend was a counterfeiter and a thief, one who was probably being hunted by lawmen all over the country. Rolf had also found thousands of dollars worth of cash, mostly in hundred-dollar bills. Rolf had no doubt in his mind that they were counterfeit, although it was obvious that his friend had taken some pains to make them appear old and hard used.

As yet, Rolf had not told either of the women about his discovery. He was hoping that Nathan's mind would clear and that his friend would take charge again and make those kinds of decisions.

"What's the name of that little settlement up ahead?'' Carole asked from the back of the buckboard, where she chose to ride beside Nathan in case he suddenly became alert and needed to speak to someone.

"I don't know,'' Rolf said. "But we must be in Arizona by now, since we already crossed the Colorado River.''

"How much did you have to pay that ferryman anyway?" Teresa asked. "He wanted a lot of money."

"It turned out he didn't really want that much," Rolf said vaguely. "Not considering all these horses and the buckboard and the swiftness of the river."

"I thought we were going to overturn for sure," Teresa said, shaking her head as if to rid it of the memory. "I don't mind telling you that I was terrified."

"Me too," Rolf admitted. "But we made it, and that's all that matters."

"That and Nathan getting well," Carole said.

"Of course," Rolf said.

Rolf was driving and Teresa was sitting beside him on the buckboard seat. The Thoroughbreds were shuffling along behind, and had grown so used to the road that Rolf didn't even bother to tie them to the wagon anymore. They just followed, partly because of the sacks of oats resting in the wagon but also because they seemed to realize that they were ill suited to survive on their own in this rugged, high-desert country. At night Rolf kept them picketed when they were camping on the trail, and he always checked their feet for stones and fed each one their grain separately. They had become as tame as little dogs, and Rolf had grown enormously fond of each animal.

"Looks like a mining town," Teresa said. "Maybe we'd be better off to circle around it. They can be pretty rough."

"I would, except that we're almost out of food and running low on grain," Rolf told her. "Besides, maybe they have a real doctor that could examine Nathan."

"Not in a little settlement like that, honey," Carole chimed in from behind. "But we really could use some

144

food, and I saw that you've taken all Nathan's money.''

Rolf flushed with embarrassment. "Carole, I didn't *steal* it! I just took what we'd need to get down to Arizona.''

"But we don't even know *where* in Arizona we're supposed to go!'' Teresa said with obvious exasperation.

"Nathan will come around,'' Rolf said, trying to sound confident. "And he'll tell us where he wanted to end up and buy a ranch.''

"But what if he *doesn't*?'' Teresa asked. "Then what do we do?''

"I don't know,'' Rolf admitted. "I've been giving that some thought, but so far I haven't come up with anything. The thing of it is, we talked a lot but he never actually said where we were going.''

"Do you think he had a specific destination in Arizona?''

Rolf shrugged. "It's hard to say. One night on the trail Nathan talked fondly of a place along the eastern slopes of the Sierra Nevada Mountains.''

"In Nevada?'' Carole asked, sounding surprised.

"I think he said it was in California.''

"Jeez,'' Teresa said, "I always wanted to see California and the ocean.''

"It'd be nice all right,'' Rolf said, "but I don't recall Nathan saying anything about any ocean nearby.''

"Well, he just must have forgot,'' Teresa said, "because California has *definitely* got an ocean. I know that for a fact because San Francisco is in California and it's beside the ocean.''

"Well then, Teresa, darling,'' Rolf said, plenty willing to concede the point as they neared the mining town, "I guess we would be close to the ocean.''

Rolf stopped the wagon and tethered the Thorough-breds together so that they could not be scattered or stolen. Then he climbed back into the buckboard and continued on. The mining settlement didn't have a name that they could locate. A lot of them had signs posted at both ends of the main street giving the name, the population, or often even the date it was founded. But this town was so hard looking that no one had bothered.

"We sure are attracting a lot of attention," Teresa said, noting the flock of miners who were beginning to stare.

"We *always* attract a lot of attention when we arrive," Carole said, cradling Nathan's head in her lap.

Rolf felt a stirring of jealousy and anger as miners, freighters, and saloon patrons stood lined along the street gawking at the new arrivals. "They act like they never seen women before," he muttered.

"Just ignore them and let's stop in front of that general store up on the right," Teresa said. "It looks to be the only one in town."

"I'll bet it's damned expensive too," Rolf grumbled.

"We've got enough money to buy anything we want," Teresa said in a low voice as she surveyed the hard, leering faces that lined the street. "Let's just buy what we need and get out of here as fast as possible."

"Good idea," Carole said.

Rolf was beginning to think that it really might have been wiser if they'd have bypassed this settlement. Other than a livery, a general store, and an assayer's office, all it had was a line of saloons, gambling halls, and other attractions created with the sole purpose of separating a miner from his gold.

Rolf tried to ignore the hard-faced men as he climbed

down from the buckboard and then handed the reins to Teresa. "I'll just grab a few things and we'll be on our way."

"Sure," she said, looking uneasy. "Just don't stray out of calling distance."

Rolf nodded, and when he started to step up upon the boardwalk, a tough-looking man blocked his view. "Whatcha doin' with them chippies, huh, kid?"

Rolf heard the mocking challenge. He felt his insides grow cold and wanted to step around the bigger man and sidestep this trouble. And he might have, but the man gave him a little shove. "I asked you a question, kid."

"Ignore him, Rolf!" Teresa said. "He's just trying to show off to his friends."

The man turned his eyes to Teresa. "You got fire. Why don't you come down here and do the women's work of shopping instead of sending the kid?"

Rolf knew that he could not avoid or win this fight. He was just not big or strong enough to whip the bully. That being the case, he had no alternative but to draw his six-gun. It came up very fast, smooth and cocked.

"Step aside," Rolf whispered, pressing the barrel of the gun to the bully's belly. "Step aside or I'll blow your guts all over the side of this building."

The bully paled. He glanced down at the pistol, then back up at Rolf and tried to sound brave. "If you kill me, kid, my friends will tear you apart."

"Fine," Rolf said. "It's a good day to die . . . but you're going to do it first."

The street fell silent. A hundred men stood watching, and not one said a word as the bully weighed the resolve in Rolf's eyes and decided that he wasn't bluffing.

"I ain't armed, kid."

"Then either get out of my sight, or get a gun," Rolf heard himself say.

"I—I was just joshin' you a little. No harm meant."

"Sure," Rolf said, prodding the man hard. "And no harm done. Now, git!"

The bully turned and hurried away. Rolf met Teresa's eyes and he thought he saw pride. But he didn't wait around to hear any more or to face another bully. Rolf stepped inside the general store and quickly began to make his purchases.

"Where you headed?" the store clerk asked, looking nervous as he hurried to fill Rolf's order.

"Maybe Prescott or Flagstaff."

"Flagstaff is a lot closer. Growin' too fast, though, since the Atlantic and Pacific Railroad passed through. They say Flagstaff is now the fastest-growin' town on the line runnin' between Albuquerque and the Pacific Coast."

"Is it surrounded by high desert sage like these parts?"

"Nope, pines. They get some pretty good snow up there."

"Ranching country?"

"Some. Prescott is better though. Not so cold and the grass has a longer growing season. You a rancher?"

"Nope. Just hopin' to be a good cowboy," Rolf admitted. "Is there a real doctor in this town?"

" 'Fraid not. People here either die or get well all on their own. Only the strong survive in Purgatory."

"Purgatory, huh." Rolf collected his goods in a burlap sack. "How much do I owe you, mister?"

"I'll tally it up."

Rolf thought he heard Teresa and she sounded angry.

"Here," he said, tossing a twenty-dollar bill on the counter. That ought to cover it."

"Why . . . why, thanks!"

Rolf hurried outside to see a man with a gun strapped on his lean hip reaching for Teresa.

"Hold it!" Rolf ordered.

The man whirled, drawing his gun so fast that Rolf didn't have time to drop his sack of provisions. And there he was, caught flat-footed and helpless.

"Mister," the gunman said with a look of triumph on his face, "you got the drop on that other fella, but I've just turned the tables on you. What are you going to do about that?"

The sack slipped out of Rolf's hand and he flexed his fingers. "Maybe I'll get off a shot," he heard himself tell the man.

"You're even stupider than you look, kid!"

Rolf wanted to draw, but he was so damned scared, he felt as if his body had turned to solid ice.

"Drop it!" Teresa ordered, cocking back the hammer of a derringer that had appeared in her little fist. "Drop it or I'll shoot you in the back, mister!"

The gunman turned and he saw not only Teresa with a derringer, but Carole also had one pointing at his chest.

"Whew!" he said, eyes falling to his own six-gun. "The odds aren't good anymore."

"Drop it," Teresa repeated.

The gunman was handsome in a lean, predatory way. He smiled and took a step toward Teresa, starting to say something, when her derringer barked smoke and flame. A red, red rose blossomed across the gunman's shoulder, and his fancy six-gun jumped from his hand as if it had a life of its own. He staggered and tried to stoop for the gun, but Teresa shot him in the knee and he went down bawling.

Rolf jumped forward and disarmed the gunman. Stuffing the man's ivory-handled six-gun into his waistband and scooping up the sack of provisions, Rolf leaped back into the buckboard.

"Have a nice day!" he called as he slapped the lines down hard on the rumps of the team and the buckboard lurched into the crowd, which parted like the Red Sea.

None of them looked back at Purgatory and they kept moving at a brisk trot until the evil little mining town was just a speck of dust on the bleak, gray horizon.

"You saved my bacon," Rolf said, taking Teresa's hand.

"Yeah, but you were brave and fast with that first fella," Teresa said proudly. "Wasn't he brave, Carole?"

"He sure was, but almost dead."

"Yeah, I was that too," Rolf said, feeling good about himself as he twisted around for about the tenth time to make sure that they were not being followed.

"Where are we going?" Carole asked.

"Flagstaff, then maybe Prescott," Rolf told her as they jounced onward in the face of a crimson and gold desert sunset.

Chapter 14

There had been a foot of snow on the ground in Flagstaff and the temperature barely got above freezing the day Rolf drove the buckboard through the northern Arizona railroad town. They found a Dr. Osmond, but he wasn't very encouraging after a cursory examination of Nathan Cox.

"I'd say the poor fellow has permanent and irreversible brain damage" was Osmond's grim prognosis.

"You're wrong!" Carole had insisted, and then they'd dragged poor Nathan out of the doctor's office and loaded him back into the buckboard.

"What now?" Rolf asked as they drove away from the doctor's office.

"Let's keep going south until we find some warmer weather," Teresa had almost begged.

Rolf thought that was a fine idea, and three blustery days later they drove into mile-high Prescott, in a lush, pine-forested valley fed by Granite Creek and surrounded on three sides by Granite Peak, Spruce Mountain, and Mount Tritle.

"Now *this* is handsome ranching country," Rolf said as they neared the old mining town famed for its riches of gold, silver, copper, and lead.

"That must be Fort Whipple over there," Carole said, pointing to a big log fort off in the distance.

"There's some pretty big cattle ranches hereabouts too," Rolf said, noting the thousands of cattle out on the winter range. "Ought to be plenty of work for a cowboy."

"If you *were* a cowboy," Teresa said. "Rolf, don't you dare be thinking about going off to find some thirty-dollar-a-month job riding fence. We're going to buy our *own* cattle ranch, remember?"

"Actually," he said, "I don't remember that agreement at all. We've no money to buy a ranch."

"Yes, we do," Carole said, looking at Teresa. "Don't you think we've both figured out what you and Nathan have hidden in those heavy packs?"

Rolf tried to sound angry. "You mean you've been snooping around in Nathan's stuff when I had my back turned?"

"Well, you snooped first!" Teresa said, looking annoyed and sliding over to the far side of the seat. "So don't you start pointing fingers at Carole and me! We know you're a couple of counterfeiters and we're willing to overlook that fact because we love you fellas. But that don't give you the right to play high and mighty."

"She's right," Carole said, nose pointing to the sky. "We found your hidden money, paper, treasury department plates, ink, and everything. Anyone could see why you and Nathan have so much money. You've been *printing* it."

"Not me!"

"Well, sure you have," Teresa said. "But don't worry, we're going to get married soon and I'll never tell."

"Just like I'm marrying Nathan and I'd never tell on him either," Carole said.

Rolf felt defensive. "Well, I'm real glad you're marryin' us, but I still didn't print any damn hundred-dollar bills. I just sort of joined up with Nathan and was hoping he'd buy a ranch and give me honest work riding fence."

"That's it?" Teresa asked.

"Yes, that's it," Rolf answered them both. "And anyway, Nathan might not want to get married. No offense, Carole, but I think you ought to wait until he's feeling better and can at least tell his own mind."

Carole was offended. "For your information, he *did* ask me to marry him."

"He did?"

"Sure! That night at the Paradise Hotel he said I was the best he'd ever had in bed and that he loved and wanted to marry me."

"Well," Rolf said, feeling much better, "if Nathan said that, then we'll all get married together in Prescott and buy a cattle ranch."

"And build two big houses and then raise big families."

Rolf glanced back into the buckboard. "You think Nathan would want a family? That he can even still *make* a family?"

"Oh, sure," Carole said, gently patting Nathan's

153

crotch. "He's still working just fine down here."

Rolf was appalled. "You . . . you did it with him since he got pistol-whipped by Clyde Zolliver?"

"We did it together three or four times already," Carole said rather proudly. "It makes Nathan smile, so I know he still likes it."

Rolf had to bite his tongue. He just wasn't sure if a man should be asked to make love to a woman if he was not right in the mind. Still, if it made Nathan smile, then what could be the harm?

Prescott wasn't as big as Flagstaff and it didn't have a railroad, but the town had a more permanent and civilized appearance that Rolf appreciated. There were a couple of churches and a Masonic hall as well as a newspaper and a one-room schoolhouse. The sign on the outskirts of Prescott said that it was the territorial capital of Arizona and that it had been founded in 1836 by Joseph Reddeford Walker and his party of mountain men.

"Look," Teresa said. "There's even a marshal's office and jail."

"That's not good," Rolf said. "Not good at all."

"Yeah, I see what you mean," Teresa said. "But we're not going to be sitting around town printing money. We're going to be printing it on our cattle ranch."

"No, we're not!" Rolf argued vehemently. "We're going to raise cattle and make an honest living at ranching."

"It's hard work," Carole warned. "I've had a lot of ranchers and cowboys, and they all were stove up with injuries from working too long and hard out in bad weather."

"The weather will be a lot better here than it was

154

where we came from," Rolf said. "This far south, they don't get such cold and blizzards."

"Do we have enough of that phony money to buy a big ranch and build a couple of big cabins?" Teresa wanted to know.

"Yep," Rolf said. "But could we talk about something else until we're out of hearing range of this town?"

"Sure," Teresa said, sliding back over to his side. "We know that spending loads of counterfeit money is a criminal offense. One that can send you to jail and even prison. That's not what Carole or I want either."

"Glad to hear that," Rolf said, spying a livery and heading in its direction. "After we put up all the horses and find rooms, we need to buy a ranch fast and get out of town before someone starts nosing around."

"Maybe there's a better doctor in this town," Carole said. "One who can really help Nathan instead of just saying he's hopeless."

"Maybe," Rolf said, but inwardly he doubted it.

An hour later, Dr. John Barry emerged from his examination room with his bushy brows knitted together. "Interesting case," he said, glancing back into the room to see Nathan just sitting zombielike on the examination table. "Your friend has definitely suffered a severe contusion or concussion."

"Doctor?" Carole asked, stepping in front of the distracted-looking physician. "Would you mind telling us what you discovered?"

Dr. Barry possessed a very large head covered with silver hair. His eyes were immense behind his thick glasses.

"Not at all," he said, removing his glasses and massaging the bridge of his nose. "To begin with, it's ob-

155

vious that your friend suffered an extremely severe blow to the anterior of his cranium about where—''

"He was pistol-whipped," Carole said very deliberately. "The blow caught Nathan just above the hairline. Are his brains scrambled, Dr. Barry?"

"Scrambled?" The doctor replaced his glasses and shook his head. "Oh, heavens, no! I happen to have taken some training in head injuries at the University of Boston and I've seen many patients recover from even more severe blows."

Carole's eyes lit up. "You mean he's going to be all right!"

"Not . . . not entirely."

Carole's smile died. "What does that mean?"

"His brain has been severely traumatized. There is cranial swelling which can be fatal."

"Fatal!" Teresa cried. "Doctor, he was injured several weeks ago."

"Oh. Then that answers my first question and puts a happier light on the matter," Barry said. "In that case, he probably won't die, but I expect that it will be a good while before his brain functions correctly again."

"What do you mean, a good while?" Rolf asked. "Weeks? Months? What?"

"A month, maybe a little longer. It's impossible to say. We just don't know enough about the brain or cranial injuries to predict. However, my experience tells me that a blow of this nature could well result in major behavioral modifications and quite likely permanent amnesia."

"Amnesia?" Teresa said. "Isn't that forgetting stuff?"

"Yes," Barry said, "it is. And in your friend's case,

it would be a permanent loss of memory.''

"*All* memory?'' Rolf asked with rising apprehension as it occurred to him that Nathan might think them strangers instead of his only friends.

"It's impossible to say,'' Barry told them. "But be warned that you might actually have to teach Nathan how to talk, feed himself, everything. On the other hand, he might remember quite a lot but with certain periods of his life missing completely. That is very common. Often, a patient will remember segments of his childhood. Special events that were either very unpleasant or very pleasant. He or she usually remembers their mother, sometimes their father or a favorite sibling.''

Dr. Barry shrugged his shoulders. "To theorize at this point is a waste of time. You will see this man begin to blink and show signs that his brain is starting to function again. Quite possibly this will happen in fits and starts. But the improvement, once it begins, will be quite dramatic.''

"What is the chance of complete recovery of his memory?'' Carole asked.

"The chances are slim to none,'' Dr. Barry said without hesitation. "I can assure you with a fair degree of certainty that this man will never completely regain his memory.''

"Will his personality be changed?'' Teresa asked.

"Most definitely. After such a trauma, most patients become more serene and even . . . I daresay . . . happier individuals. They may lack a high degree of concentration ability, but they seem to enjoy life to an extent that most of us could never even hope to achieve.''

"A mixed blessing,'' Rolf mused aloud.

"Yes," Barry agreed, overhearing the remark, "definitely mixed."

The doctor turned to Carole. "Didn't you introduce yourself to me as his fiancée when you first came into my office?"

"Yes."

"Then your patience will be sorely tried at times and you will question if this is even the same man that you chose to marry. But I promise you, miss, that Nathan will eventually make a strong recovery and become an absolute delight. You must simply be loving and patient."

"I've been loving him plenty already, and when I do it, he really gets excited and smiles a lot," Carole explained, looking quite pleased.

The doctor blushed. "Well," he said, recovering nicely, "go easy on the 'loving' part for a while. This man is recuperating, and it might not be wise to overtax his . . . his most basic functions."

"Huh?"

"Just lay off his body for a few weeks," Teresa said, "isn't that what you're trying to say, Doctor?"

"Exactly," the man replied, turning away and removing a stethoscope from his neck, then pretending to arrange his tray of instruments.

Rolf paid the doctor and they led Nathan outside. He looked around the town, and then he actually nodded his head and a faint smile played at the corners of his mouth.

"Look at him," Carole said, hugging Nathan's arm, "my love thinks the doctor's advice about us not doing it was every bit as ridiculous as I did!"

"Or," Teresa said, "he recognizes things here in Prescott and they bring back good memories."

"There's a land office up the street," Rolf said, shouldering a pair of saddlebags heavy with counterfeit hundred-dollar bills. "Let's go buy a ranch."

The land office was staffed by just one man, a very jolly and heavyset fellow who introduced himself as Albert A. Atherton.

"But you can call me Big Al," he said, motioning them all to chairs in his tiny office but obviously having a difficult time keeping from staring at Nathan.

Finally, Al said, "His face is very familiar. Isn't he . . . isn't that Nathan Cox?"

"Yes," Teresa said before Rolf could think of some alias that might help to protect them.

"I *knew* it!" Al said. "The rest of the family left here a couple years back. I heard they went down to Tucson and started raising sheep in the desert. I don't know that for a fact though. What's wrong with Nathan anyway? Why doesn't he say something instead of just staring at the floor?"

"He's grown quite shy since leaving Arizona," Rolf said, not wanting to go into a long explanation that would only lead to further questions that could be detrimental to all their futures. "We have cash and we want to buy a cattle ranch."

"Cash, huh!" Al actually rubbed his fat hands together. "Well, cash always talks! How much cash and how much of a ranch do you want to buy?"

Before Rolf could tell the man that they had about twenty thousand dollars, Teresa said, "What kinds of good ranches are available?"

"Actually," Al said, "the old Cox homestead is up for sale. Big ranch with about four thousand acres of excellent land, timber, and grass. Six water-holding ponds that will save your beef in the fall when Granite Creek gets low, and even a couple of silver mines that still haven't produced but that could someday.''

"How much?" Rolf asked, knowing in a flash that this was the ranch that Nathan would want.

"Asking price is twelve thousand dollars."

"Twelve thousand!" Teresa exclaimed.

"That's just the *asking* price," Al said quickly. "I suspect that you could get it for . . . oh, about nine— cash.''

"What kind of buildings does it come with?" Carole asked.

"Why, Nathan can tell you that," Al said, staring at Nathan, who kept staring at the floor.

"Why don't *you* tell us," Rolf said.

"All right. The Cox ranch has a big main ranch house with a veranda and cellar for roots and potatoes, apples and such. Then it has another smaller but nicer log cabin with four rooms and a fine stone fireplace. There are barns, a toolshed, blacksmith shop, and tack rooms. Comes with some wagons and harness. The land is completely fenced with three strands of wire and good cedar posts. There are four wells, the best right at the house and—''

"We'll take it," Rolf said, reaching for the saddlebags and the counterfeit money.

"Well!" Al said, rubbing his hands together. "We need to sign some documents over at the bank and then we can settle this today.''

"Good," Rolf said, "but we also want to be married.''

"Today?"

"Right now," Carole said, "before we sign the papers as joint owners."

Rolf started to object because the counterfeit money really belonged to Nathan, but then he realized it really didn't. The counterfeit money didn't belong to anyone, or at least it wasn't supposed to have any value to anyone.

"I expect that we can find a preacher at the church," Teresa said, grabbing Rolf by the arm and practically dragging him out the door.

"His name is Deacon Ward!" Al called. "Just pay him up front and we'll all meet at the bank in fifteen minutes. Okay?"

"Okay!" Teresa called back as Carole hustled poor Nathan out the door and caught up with them.

The wedding took only ten minutes. Signing all the papers in order to buy the old Cox ranch and then opening an account with the Bank of Prescott took nearly two hours. But it was worth it. All four rode out in the buckboard, grinning like mad fools. And the best part was yet to come, when they took over the old ranch, spent their first nights as husband and wives, then began the job of cattle ranching, providing the place came with some cows.

As far as Rolf was concerned, this whole thing was just a miracle, a dream come true. It was hard to believe that less than a month ago he was riding with outlaws who treated him like dirt and called him a snot-nosed kid.

Chapter 15

"You want to wait outside or come in with me?" Longarm asked Diana one cold afternoon as they reined in
before the Purgatory, Arizona, general store.

Diana looked around at the rough citizenry. "I think
I'd rather stick close to you," she quickly decided.

Longarm followed her eyes and read her concerns.
"Probably a real good idea," he said, dismounting and
tying his horse and then Diana's to the hitching rail.

"Afternoon!" the clerk behind the counter said in
greeting. "What can I help you with today?"

"Thought we'd stay over tonight in the hotel just up
the street, then come back here in the morning and buy
some provisions."

The clerk measured Diana and smiled, then turned to
Longarm and said, "I'm a little afraid that our hotel
might not be to the lady's liking."

"Why not?"

"Things get pretty wild at night over there."

"What's the alternative?" Diana asked.

The clerk grinned even wider. "I was hoping you'd ask. Why don't you both take room and board tonight in my home? My wife cooks a mean chicken and dumplings and I'll guarantee that you won't be bothered by our local rowdies."

Longarm knew that Diana was worn out and decided that he ought to accept the offer. "All right," Longarm said, "but how much a night?"

"Five dollars for the two of you and that includes dinner, a big breakfast, and a place to put up your horses where they won't get stolen. I grain 'em and feed 'em well right along with my own horses."

"Private bedroom?"

"Of course," the clerk said. "And the walls are pretty thick so . . . well, so you can sleep as late as you like."

"We'll accept your offer," Longarm said, "as long as it comes with a hot bath."

"Why, sure, but it's cash in advance."

Longarm started to dig into his pockets. He'd broken a hundred-dollar bill in Whiskey Creek so he wouldn't even be paying this fella counterfeit money.

"First," he said, pausing with his hand in his pocket, "we could use a little information."

"Then you come to the right place."

"We're looking for a couple of men and their lady friends. They were traveling in a buckboard with some fine Thoroughbred horses, and I wouldn't be surprised if they stopped here for provisions."

The clerk leaned forward, elbows on his counter. "What'd they look like?"

"One man was handsome, but he's been pistol-whipped and might have been either unconscious or feeling poorly. The other was a kid barely out of his teens.''

"I remember that bunch! The kid seemed to be the one in charge, and I do recollect that a pair stayed in the rear of the buckboard.''

"When did they pass through this settlement?'' Diana asked.

"A couple of days ago. They raised some eyebrows here, I'll tell you!''

"Why?''

"They had some trouble right out here in front of my store.''

"What kind of trouble?''

"It was quite a sight! You see, a local gunnie named Fred Stillwell tried to buffalo the kid and got a couple of bullets for his trouble.''

"The kid shot him?'' Diana asked.

"Nope. The woman beside the kid shot Fred with her derringer. Hit him once in the knee and once in the shoulder. Fred got septic fever and died last night.''

"And then?'' Longarm asked.

"Then they all climbed back in that buckboard with the provisions just like they were going off on a damned Sunday picnic and drove south out of town.''

"South?'' Longarm wanted to be very clear on this point. "Not east?''

"South for sure.''

Longarm frowned. "I thought sure they'd be turning west by now in order to go into the desert country and try to shake any pursuit. Maybe they really are going to Prescott.''

"To me it makes a lot of sense,'' Diana said. "If Nathan is hurt as bad as we're starting to think, the

Swensen kid and those Whiskey Creek girls would be hoping that there were a few of his relatives left in Prescott that might be able to help them.''

"Yeah," Longarm said, glancing up suddenly at the clerk. "Did they pay you with a hundred-dollar bill?"

"Nope. They gave me a twenty."

"Glad to hear that," Longarm said, turning to leave.

"Hey, what about your room?"

"We'd better push on," Longarm said, speaking to Diana. "At least until dark."

She sighed. "All right, but I am sick to death of sleeping on the trail."

The clerk came around and said, "Folks, it's too late to start out on the trail this evening."

"We got a little sunlight left."

"Why freeze tonight on the ground when you know that you'll find those people in Flagstaff or Prescott?"

"Good question," Diana said.

"Of course it is!" the clerk said. "You'd both be a lot better off to stay over tonight, get a good night's sleep, and then push on tomorrow morning after one of my wife's big old breakfasts of sourdough biscuits, bacon, and buttermilk."

"Custis, please?" Diana asked.

"All right," he said, digging five dollars out of his pants. "I guess it'll be dark pretty soon anyways."

"Could rain too," the clerk said, taking the money and then giving them directions to his house. "Supper is at seven. Wife likes you to be at the dining table on time. She'll make it worth your while."

"We'll do that," Longarm promised as they started for the front door. "And, Diana, we'll be leaving early."

"Then I'll want a *full* night's sleep," Diana said pointedly.

"Fine," Longarm told her. "I could use one too."

The store clerk winked and grinned but had the good sense not to say anything before Longarm and Diana left.

True to his promise, the bed had been soft, the sheets clean, and the food excellent in Purgatory. And after reaching Flagstaff, Longarm found Dr. Osmond, who had very little good to say about Nathan Cox.

"I told them the man was brain damaged and not to expect very much in the way of recovery."

"It's that bad, huh?" Longarm said.

"Well, I'm not really a doctor," Osmond admitted. "But I have read some medical books and seen quite a few men with head injuries. This fella in the buckboard was hurt pretty bad. Most of them like that never fully recover."

Longarm and Diana exchanged glances, then Longarm turned back to Osmond and said, "Thanks for your information."

"Good luck catching them, Marshal."

That same hour they resupplied their provisions and pushed on for Prescott.

A short way south of town Diana said, "You know I'm bitter about the way that Nathan lied and cheated me. But I have to tell you that I feel bad that he might never recover. I just can't quite imagine him being permanently helpless."

"It's sad," Longarm said, watching a train as it puffed into town. "I've never inflicted that kind of damage on anyone, but it happens."

"If Nathan was in charge, he'd never return to Prescott," Diana said. "He'd realize Prescott was the first place we'd look for him. This can mean only that Nathan is incapable of making decisions."

"And counterfeit money," Longarm added, "which is the only bright side to this sad business."

"Yes," Diana said, "I hadn't thought of that. I know nothing about the subject, but I suppose it's unlikely that either of the two women or the kid would have the knowledge and skill to make counterfeit money."

"Completely unlikely," Longarm agreed. "It would be easy work for a skilled printer, but not for a would-be cowboy and a couple of saloon girls."

"I almost feel sorry for the way they've been caught up in this web," Diana said. "Must you arrest Swensen and the women?"

"Probably," Longarm said as they rode out of Flagstaff, "but I doubt that any charges will stick unless they actually try to use the plates. Their obvious defense would be to claim that they didn't know about the plates or the counterfeit money."

"But they've been spending it."

"So have we," Longarm reminded her, "as well as everyone else who has taken in that bogus money. It would be a waste of time to arrest those three. They'd beat any charges filed against them in court."

"I can't say that I would feel too bad about that," Diana confessed.

"No more burning revenge?"

"Not for the kid or the women."

"What about for Nathan?"

Diana gave the question some thought before she answered. "I can't forgive him," she finally said, "but

167

how can you hate someone who has been robbed of their mind?''

''I don't know. What if the doctor was wrong and he managed a full recovery?''

''Then he'd deserve prison . . . or worse, for killing his accomplice.''

''I agree,'' Longarm said, feeling a sudden icy blast of wind strike him full in the face. Longarm pulled his sheepskin collar up to cover his cheeks and ears. ''It's cold up here in these pines.''

''Is Prescott warmer?''

''Yes,'' Longarm said, ''because it's lower and farther south.''

Diana touched her heels to the flanks of her mare. ''Then let's hurry up,'' she said, ''because I am beginning to feel like a big icicle!''

Longarm pushed his horse into an easy gallop and he turned his thoughts to Prescott. It had been several years since he'd seen that mining town, and he supposed that it had grown like most settlements in the Arizona Territory.

Chapter 16

When Longarm and Diana reached the old Arizona mining town of Prescott, the first stop they made was at the marshal's office. Unfortunately, there was a sign on his door saying that he had gone elk hunting for a few days and that if there was any trouble, to contact Mayor Jesse Taylor three doors down on the right.

"We're not going to wait for the marshal to return from hunting," Longarm said, "and we're not going to trouble the mayor about the federal government's missing property and this counterfeiting business."

"Then how will we find Nathan and the rest?" Diana asked.

"We'll ask a few questions," Longarm said, looking up and down the street. "The livery is a good place to start, as well as the general store, because they'd most likely be out of provisions, same as us."

"What about that doctor's office?" Diana asked, pointing just up the street.

"I think that would also be an excellent place to start," Longarm agreed. "Let's go."

Dr. Barry was not the most cooperative man Longarm had ever interviewed, even after the physician had examined his badge.

"Mr. Cox has been in twice since my initial examination," Dr. Barry finally revealed. "His prognosis is guarded, but we're quite optimistic that he will regain most of his mental functions and about sixty percent of his memory. But that's just a guess and you should know that it's quite impossible to say with any real degree of accuracy."

"Where is Cox right now?"

Barry hesitated. "Why are you seeking this man?"

"It's a federal matter."

"Is he a criminal?" Barry asked.

Longarm had no intention of telling the doctor anything. "We need to speak with Cox as well as his friends. Now, Dr. Barry, will you help, or do I have to start asking questions and raising eyebrows all over Prescott?"

Barry removed his thick glasses. "Marshal Long, if you really are *that* determined, I probably ought to cooperate."

"Excellent idea. Where can we find them?"

Dr. Barry quickly told Longarm and Diana about how Rolf Swensen and the two women had bought the old Cox ranch. "I hear they paid nine thousand dollars for it—cash! But even that was a good buy according to people who know the cattle market and the property itself, which, I understand, has enormous potential not only for ranching, but also for its timber and mineral rights.''

Diana smiled. ''I'll bet they paid for it in hundred-dollar bills.''

''Beg your pardon?''

''Never mind.''

''How do we get to the Cox ranch?'' Longarm asked.

Dr. Barry gave them directions and ended by saying, ''You can't miss the place when you come to that big pile of boulders west of town.''

''Thanks,'' Longarm said. ''What kind of shape was Nathan Cox in the last time you saw him?''

''That was just yesterday,'' Barry said, ''and he was showing a tremendous amount of improvement. He was walking and eating well, his eyes were in focus, and he seemed much more alert.''

Diana pushed forward, ''Does he remember *anything* about the past?''

''No,'' Barry said, ''and his wife told me—''

''Wife?'' Diana asked with surprise.

''Yes,'' Dr. Barry said, ''her name is Carole. She is very devoted to Nathan and is, I think, largely responsible for his excellent care and dramatic improvement.''

''Humph!''

''Do you . . . do you know the woman?'' Dr. Barry asked.

''No,'' Diana said.

Barry replaced his glasses on his beak and eyed Longarm suspiciously. ''I trust that you're not going to *arrest* any of those fine people, are you, Marshal?''

Longarm took Diana's arm and pointed her toward the door. ''Thank you very much for your help, Dr. Barry.''

The physician herded them out his door. ''I would be

lying if I said that you were welcome, Marshal Long.''

"He knows that this isn't a social call we're about to make," Diana said as they headed for their horses.

"Diana, I really would prefer you to stay here in town while I—''

"Not on your life! Do you think that I have come this far and endured so much to be shut out now?''

"No," Longarm said, "I suppose not.''

"Well, you're damn right I haven't!" she said. "I may not have the same motive, to kill Nathan, but I still want my money back.''

"Of course," Longarm said, untying his reins and then wearily mounting his horse.

"I'm glad that you're so understanding," Diana said as she also mounted. "Now, let's go put an end to this whole sorry business.''

They had no trouble finding the Cox ranch. Longarm even spotted the Thoroughbreds grazing in a big pasture near the ranch house.

"How are you going to handle this?" Diana asked. "You know that the kid is quick on the trigger and that the two Whiskey Creek women are dangerous as hell.''

"Yes," Longarm said, "I know that. I think that I should just ride in alone. Nathan might still recognize you, but he's never seen me.''

"Bad idea!''

"*Good* idea," Longarm said firmly. "If something goes wrong, you can ride for help.''

"And do what?" she asked. "Find out where Prescott's marshal went elk hunting?''

"Please," Longarm said patiently. "Just do as I ask for this once. Stay back here in the trees. If everything goes as it should, I'll signal and you can ride in then.''

Diana didn't like the idea, but she could see that Longarm was quite serious. "All right," she said at last, "we'll do it your way. But I'll be watching from cover, and if anything goes amiss, I'm coming to your rescue."

"Okay," Longarm agreed.

Diana leaned out of her saddle and gave him a kiss. "After tonight," she said, "I vote we take a few weeks off and find even warmer weather. We can have some fun together and relax. What do you say?"

"Sounds good," Longarm said, "but there could be a problem with my boss back in Denver as well as the mayor and—"

"To hell with them!" Diana touched his cheek. "What have they done for us lately? Nothing. They never even wired you legitimate travel expense money."

"That's true," Longarm admitted as he reined toward the ranch headquarters.

They were all sitting in front of a big stone fireplace playing penny-ante poker, laughing and sipping on whiskey, when Longarm tied his horse up in front of the ranch house and simply walked inside.

"Hey!" Rolf exclaimed, jumping to his feet. "Who the hell are you to just walk in here?"

Longarm studied the two women, then Nathan, who was still smiling, and he decided to draw his gun and give them the bad news.

"I'm United States Deputy Marshal Custis Long," he said, reaching into his coat pocket and dragging out his badge. "And I hate to ruin this party, but you're all under arrest."

"On what charges!" Carole cried.

"They'll vary depending on how much you cooperate," Longarm answered. "Now, everyone stand up and turn around slowly with your hands over your heads."

"You can't do this without telling us what we're being charged with!" Teresa said angrily.

"All right, passing counterfeit money, aiding and abetting a criminal and fugitive of the law."

"We didn't do anything of those things!" Carole protested.

"That will be decided later," Longarm said. "And on top of all that, you gals shot and killed a man in Whiskey Creek."

"That gunnie was going to kill us!" Rolf cried.

Longarm turned his complete attention on Rolf. "What about Clyde Zolliver?"

"He was another that gave us no choice," Rolf said. "It was him . . . or us."

"Well," Longarm said, "all I know for sure right now is that you've left a path of counterfeit money in your wake along with two dead men. And I'm quite sure that you bought this ranch with bad money."

Rolf sighed. "Look, Marshal, those two men that we shot were trying to kill us. There are witnesses."

"I've spoken to them."

"Then you know that we killed in self-defense," Carole said.

"Maybe."

"Marshal, if you'd—"

"Hands up," Longarm ordered, "and turn around. Now!"

The three did as they were told, but Nathan Cox didn't do anything except look confused.

"Who are you?" he asked as Longarm made sure that the kid and the two women were unarmed. "Do you want to play cards with us?"

"Glad to finally meet you, Nathan Cox?"

"That's what they call me," Nathan said. "Are you hungry, mister?"

"I am, but food can wait."

"No, no! I'll get something," Nathan said, heading for the kitchen.

Longarm just let the man go. Not even a professional actor could have faked the blank expression on Cox's handsome face or the genuine need to be of service.

"Sit down," Longarm ordered the three after checking to make sure they had no hideout weapons.

"You can't take my husband all the way back to Denver," Carole said.

Before Longarm could arrange his thoughts and pose a first question, Nathan came back with a tray of milk and cookies. "I baked them just like Mommy showed me how," he said happily.

Longarm took a couple and so did the others. They were oatmeal cookies and damned good.

"If you take my husband back to Denver," Carole said, "they'll put him in a prison and he'll be at the mercy of the other prisoners. At best, they'll ridicule Nathan and make him their slave. At worst . . . well, you can see that he now has a child's innocence, and you know what would become of him living among hardened criminals, Marshal Long."

"Yes," Longarm said, "but I don't have the authority to exonerate him from all the crimes he's committed. And he did kill his Denver accomplice."

"Who tried to kill him first!" Carole cried.

"Is that what Nathan said?" Longarm asked.

"Yes, and I believe him. They got in a fight and Nathan won."

"I've got to take you all back to Denver," Longarm said. "After that, what happens is up to the court system."

"They'll want to imprison Nathan," Carole said. "And probably us as well."

"Possibly."

Longarm sat down in a chair. "But as for those two men who you killed, I am convinced that you did so in self-defense. Especially when you, Mr. Swensen, gunned down Clyde Zolliver in that upstairs hotel hallway."

Teresa stood up. "And what about all this? We have a fine ranch now. It has helped Nathan to recover. To regain his happiest childhood memories. We're sure that he can be happy here and that we can all repay society many times over for the damage we've caused."

"I'm sorry," Longarm said, "but you need to tell that to a judge, not to me."

"I could make some more cookies," Nathan interrupted. "It wouldn't take long."

"No thanks," Longarm said.

"Why do you have that thing in your hand?" Nathan asked innocently.

"It's a gun," Longarm explained, holstering the weapon.

"And what does it do?"

"It shoots bullets."

Nathan turned to his wife. "What are bullets, dear Carole?"

"You don't really want to know."

Nathan nodded and turned back to Longarm. "You look hungry, so I *am* going to make more of my mother's cookies."

"Thanks," Longarm said as the man shuffled away.

"You can't do this to Nathan," Carole whispered in a trembling voice.

"I am sworn to uphold the law," Custis heard himself reply. "And so we'll be leaving first thing in the morning."

"And the ranch?" Rolf asked. "We bought cattle and they're going to be delivered next week. And I hired a couple of *real* cowboys and we're going to—"

"You had no right to do any of that," Longarm said, cutting the kid off in mid-sentence before he went to the front door, stuck his arm outside, and fired his six-gun.

As expected, Diana came on the run.

"Who is she?" Carole asked.

"A friend of mine," Longarm answered, "and a former acquaintance of your husband."

A icy veil of suspicion dropped over Carole's eyes. "Just make sure that she stays away from my Nathan."

"No problem," Custis said a moment before Diana hurried inside.

Longarm would never forget the sight a few moments later when Diana Frank saw Nathan standing in the kitchen making cookie dough and humming some childlike little song from his boyhood. A small cry was torn from Diana's mouth as she whirled and ran right back out the front door, weeping.

"What's wrong with her?" Rolf asked, looking confused.

"She loved him," Carole said, her face no longer hard. "It's clear to see that she loved my Nathan."

"Yeah," Longarm said quietly, "and I'm not too sure she doesn't still."

177

Chapter 17

Longarm woke up at dawn the next morning. After dressing and starting a fire for coffee, he went outside to grain the horses in preparation for a long trip back to Colorado. He had not slept well during the night and felt a little groggy. The way Longarm figured it, the best and easiest way to return to Denver would be to go to Flagstaff, take an eastbound train to Albuquerque, and then make his final destination plans.

The kid had told Longarm where to find the stolen Denver mint plates as well as the currency paper and ink. The three fugitives had decided to hide everything in the barn under some hay. Longarm had pretty well decided to destroy the government currency plates and burn the paper rather than to have to worry about their safe transfer back to Colorado.

The air was clear and cold. The sun was just peeking over the eastern horizon when Longarm stopped outside the barn to admire the sunrise. He was yawning when he thought he heard something move behind him, but before he could react, Buck Zolliver stepped out of the barn, gun up and trained on Longarm's chest.

"Well, Mister Lawman," Buck said, his eyes burning with hatred. "I guess it's finally payback time for you, huh?"

Longarm felt a chill pass through his body. "Maybe."

"Why don't you turn around and enjoy your last sunrise. I'll give you about a minute's worth."

"If you shoot me, you'll wake up everyone in the house," Longarm said, trying desperately to give himself time to think of a way to get the drop on this hateful giant.

"Lawman, I'm not worried about 'em."

"Neither was Clyde, and I expect that's why he was gunned down in that hotel back in Whiskey Creek. Are you going to make the same mistake?"

Buck's eyes narrowed. "Where's the kid?"

"In bed asleep, I expect."

"And all that counterfeit money and those government plates?"

"I dunno," Longarm drawled. "I forgot to ask."

"Liar!"

Buck cocked back the hammer on his six-gun. "I ain't gonna play any games. Where are they at?"

"The plates or the money?" Longarm asked.

"Both!"

"The kid said that they're hidden in the barn under some hay. I was just about to look for them myself."

"Reach down with your left hand and ease that hogleg out of its holster," Buck ordered. "Let it drop to the ground and step away from it real slow."

Longarm saw no choice but to do as he was told. Buck picked up his Colt and shoved it into his waistband.

"Now, Marshal, step inside," Buck ordered, swinging open both of the barn doors. "And shot or no shot, if you make one false move, I'll drill you in the guts and then I'll kill all three of them in the house. Clyde was naked and unarmed when the kid gunned him down. It won't be the same this time."

"I expect it wouldn't be," Longarm said.

"Inside!"

Longarm went inside, body tight and ready to spring at Buck if he lowered his guard even a little. But the giant never gave him a chance to attack, so Longarm stopped in the middle of the barn.

"Now what?" he asked.

"Find the gawddamn money and counterfeiting plates!"

Longarm knew where to look, but he acted as if he didn't have a clue and began to rummage around in the straw, poking and prodding, even hoping that he could locate a pitchfork or any damn weapon that he could whip around and throw at Buck just long enough to make a dive for the giant's legs. If he could get the man down, he'd have a fighting chance. Hell, he'd whipped Buck once and he figured that he could do it again.

"Hurry up!" Buck raged. "Dammit, quit playing games!"

Longarm heard the anger and knew that he could not delay any longer. So he found Nathan's canvas packs and pulled them out in the open, then knocked off the loose straw.

"Here you are, Buck."

"Open 'em!"

Longarm opened the packs. One of them had a lot of counterfeit currency. He grabbed a handful and raised it for the gunman to see. "I expect this is what you're *really* after."

Buck grinned. "You got that right. And I'll use some of it to find the best printer in the country. He can make me some more."

"Got it all figured out, huh?"

"You bet I do! I've had plenty of time."

Longarm was about to say something, when he saw a shadow in the doorway and then Nathan appeared. He was smiling and said, "Good morning, everyone, I—"

Buck whipped around and fired in one smooth motion. Nathan spun and fell and before Buck could pivot back. Longarm had already drawn his hidden two-shot .44-caliber derringer that he always kept attached to his Ingersol railroad watch chain and concealed in his vest pocket. The derringer had saved his life on more than one desperate occasion, and it did the same now as Longarm sent both bullets into Buck's thick chest.

But even with two bullets, Buck somehow managed to stay on his feet long enough to fire a shot that went just wide of Longarm, who threw himself at the dying man's legs and tackled him to the ground.

Longarm drew back his fist to smash the man, but Buck heaved a deep sigh and breathed no more.

"Nathan!" Longarm said, jumping to his feet. "Nathan, are you all right!"

Nathan was *not* all right, but the bullet had only grazed his arm. He lay on his back, whimpering, and when Longarm used his bandanna to tie up the wound, Nathan blubbered, "I don't like guns!"

Longarm helped Nathan to his feet. He heard the front

door to the house slam open and knew that more help was on the way.

"Oh, to hell with it!" Longarm swore after Dr. Barry had examined Nathan and pronounced that he was suffering from shock.

"What does that mean?" Diana said.

"It means that I'm going to destroy the Denver mint's stolen goods and then we're riding out of here and leaving these people alone."

Diana's face lit up. "We are!"

"Yes."

"But I thought that you said—"

"Yeah," Longarm agreed, "I did say a lot of things last night about how the courts needed to sort all this out. But I didn't sleep well on that talk, and now that Nathan has saved my life and taken the bullet meant for me, I'd sleep on it even worse. So I'm destroying the plates and what's left of the counterfeit money and then we're riding for Albuquerque."

"But what will happen to these people!" Diana said, looking at Rolf, Teresa, Carole, and Nathan.

"I dunno," Longarm said, "but I expect that they'd better learn to become ranchers."

Diana threw her arms around Longarm and began kissing him. Rolf and the two women from Whiskey Creek began hugging and dancing around in the yard. Longarm's eyes met those of Dr. Barry, and the physician nodded as an understanding passed between them. Buck's death would be their secret, and he'd be buried quietly on this ranch. Nothing would ever be said, not even to the local marshal.

Longarm yawned mightily, prompting Diana to say, "What's the matter, sleepy?"

"As a matter of fact, I am."

"Come on," she said, taking his hand, "I'm going to tuck you right back into bed."

He grinned. "Yeah, but am I going to have a chance to sleep?"

"Maybe later," Diana said with a wink as they shuffled through the crimson glow of sunrise toward the ranch house.

Watch for

LONGARM AND THE MINUTE MEN

213th novel in the bold LONGARM series
from Jove

Coming in September!

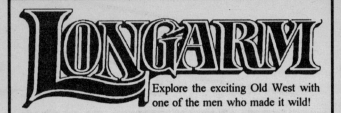